The Mystery Boys

Inca Gold

Van Powell

Alpha Editions

This edition published in 2024

ISBN : 9789361476181

Design and Setting By
Alpha Editions
www.alphaedis.com
Email - info@alphaedis.com

Contents

CHAPTER I
A DEAD LETTER COMES TO LIFE

The whole mysterious affair puzzled Cliff. To have those queer strangers appear suddenly at Aunt Lucy's with their unusual questions threw him a little off his stride.

"No," he answered the stocky Spaniard with the crafty, shifty eyes, "I did not get a letter from Peru. Who wrote it? Is it from my father? How do you know about it?"

While the Spaniard interpreted the answer to his companion Cliff studied them both. If the tall, stalwart man with copper skin and piercing eyes was not an Indian, Cliff had never seen a truthful picture of one. He wore European clothes but he was not at his ease in them. While he listened to the queer language which the Spaniard used he kept his eyes boring Cliff and Cliff saw that his denial was not believed.

Copper-skin muttered something and the Spaniard turned again to Cliff.

"You not get letter? *Mi amigo*, my friend, say it mail 'nine, ten week' ago."

"I can't help that," Cliff declared, "It hasn't come. Who is it from—my father?" Cliff had not heard from his father in nearly five years: naturally he was anxious about the scholar who studied ancient civilizations and who had gone to Peru to write a book about the Incas.

"Letter from man you not know." The Spaniard was very impressive; he spoke slowly, "When it come you not open it. You give to us *pronto*! We pay much money."

"Why?" demanded Cliff, "What is in the letter?"

The Spaniard turned and began exchanging words with the Indian. Cliff, sitting with his chums, Nicky and Tom, on Aunt Lucy's cottage porch, looked at his friends helplessly. They, staring with wide eyes, showed plainly that they could not help him with his puzzle. A letter from Peru; from a man he did not know! It must be delivered to these strangers unopened. They would pay well for it. Why? What was it all about?

Clifford Gray was as clean-cut a youth of fifteen as any of the several hundred who attended Amadale Military Academy, in this suburb of a thriving mid-Western city. He was not handsome but he had clear, direct, observant eyes, a firm, almost stubborn chin and a cheerful grin; his body was well built and kept in splendid trim by much athletic activity. That he was calm, cool, in full control of his finely muscled arms was proved on the day that the Amadale baseball pitcher "blew up" in the fourth inning of an important game, letting two runs come in and filling two bases by "walking" a pair of the opposing team; Cliff went in to pitch, with one man out. After two wild balls that clipped the corner of the plate, he surprised the confident batsman with swift pitches which rapped the catcher's glove as the bat swung, and fine, teasing curves that broke just too soon to be hit. After holding the opposing runs where they were for the next five innings he drove in the tying run and himself scored the needed one to win and became a hero in Amadale.

He lived with his Aunt Lucy because his father traveled in distant lands, studying old ruins for his histories of ancient people. Aunt Lucy took a few "boarders" and mothered the boys without coddling them. Among her "boarders" Tom and Nicky were favorites. Tom was a quiet, thoughtful youth just a month older than Cliff; Nicky, talkative and full of spirits, was the youngest of the trio. All three were drawn together by a common bond; each had a mystery in his life. Cliff's mystery seemed in a fair way to become very much alive.

The Spaniard and his companion had reached some agreement. Cliff, his eyes missing nothing, his brain alert, surmised from the stocky foreigner's shifting glance that he was about to say something either wholly or partly untrue.

"I tell you," he stated to Cliff, "it look to you—how you say!—funny, eh? I make you see."

"*Mi amigo*—this friend, he live in Quito, that place was once great Peruvian city of Inca people." Cliff nodded. He knew something about Quito, capital of an empire conquered by the Incas before the Spaniards, in their turn, conquered them.

"*Si! Si.* You *sabe* Quito. White man come there—five year' ago. Ask this *amigo* to guide to old ruins."

"My father!" declared Cliff, eagerly, while Tom and Nicky sat forward on the porch swing, intent and excited.

"*Quien sabe*—who knows? I think yes. This man agree to take white man to old ruins in cordillerras—mountains! They stop in village where is—how you say?—festival of wedding.

"White man get very drunk. He have fight and shoot natives."

To Cliff that did not ring true; his father was a quiet man, not the sort to take much wine or to use firearms except in self defense. However, he said nothing.

"One native die," went on the Spaniard, "Others very angry. Put white man in prison. He think they kill him. He write letter and ask this friend of me, here, to escape away and send letter. This man must swim in river to escape.

Water make the address of letter so it is not to send." He made a gesture of smudging ink and flung out his hands to indicate helplessness.

"This friend not know what to do. He not read. He put letter away and forget. He learn after 'while the white man kill' by natives."

Cliff was saddened by the story, even though he had no proof that it really concerned his father. Tom and Nicky looked sorrowful and sympathetic.

"Ten week ago," the Spaniard continued, "this man see another white man in mountains, make hunt for the place of gold mining."

"A prospector," Nicky interrupted. Cliff nodded.

"This man ask white man about letter, what to do. I am in camp with white man, *Americano*. But I not read letter. Other one do that and grin and laugh and take new envelop' and put on address from inside letter. He go away and mail at Cuzco.

"Then——" he was very impressive. "He tell me letter say this friend of me is one who lead other white man to death!"

That explained why they were so anxious to see the letter, of course. It might not be a letter from his father—but who else in Peru knew him or knew his address? But his father would not get into a brawl. Perhaps he did write that he was led into danger. In that case the Indian was guilty of it.

"The letter has not arrived," Cliff repeated.

"Maybe it went to the Dead Letter Office," Nicky suggested. "Maybe the other fellow didn't address it right."

The Spaniard did not interpret this; evidently he did not understand, not being familiar with American postal systems.

"White man dead—not letter" he corrected. Cliff smiled.

"We can't do anything until it comes," he said, "Then——"

"You give to us?" eagerly. "You not open. We pay——"

"I won't promise anything like that," Cliff shook his head, Tom and Nicky doing likewise. "But I will promise not to open it until you are here. That's fair, isn't it?"

When the Spaniard had interpreted, his companion said something that made the interpreter laugh with a vicious glint in his eyes.

At the same instant Nicky laid an excited hand on Cliff's arm. All of them saw the direction of his intent gaze and turned to look.

The postman was coming along the suburban street, chatting with this one and that one as he delivered mail. His mission was clear to the foreigners and they stood waiting, tense and eager. Those were mild poses compared to the suspense of the three chums. They almost trembled in their excitement.

At their gate their jolly letter carrier waved something at Cliff.

"I declare," Cliff, eyes fixed on him, heard him banter. "How did you ever get you a girl so far away? Why, it would cost you a year's allowance to go and call on her!"

He skimmed a fat missive toward the porch. Cliff ran half way down the steps and caught it. From above him, the others stared. There was no mistaking that unusual stamp.

The letter was from Peru.

CHAPTER II
THE MYSTERY BOYS ADD A MEMBER

As Cliff came up the steps with his Peruvian letter both strangers acted together; each made a grab. Cliff stopped.

"Look here!" he challenged, "You wait until I open this!"

He put the letter behind him. They saw that on the steps he was in a position to turn and elude them. Retreating a step the Spaniard nodded and the Indian stood aside, his arms folded. Tom and Nicky were already beside Cliff, ready to help him.

Flanking him they accompanied him as he mounted to the porch and faced the men. The chums formed a tableau; it might have been called "United we stand."

But they held the pose for only an instant! As they passed him the Indian, with catlike agility, moved back and then stepped down to the point Cliff had just vacated. He, then, was on the steps. They saw that they had lost a point of strategic advantage for the Indian blocked the way of escape to the yard.

Cliff, about to strip open the letter, paused.

"What are you trying to do?" he demanded.

He discovered the answer at once. The Spaniard made a spring toward Cliff, hand reaching, fingers clutching at the letter. The Indian opened his arms to block any leap toward the steps and Cliff saw that he was almost trapped. But not quite!

Nicky stuck out a foot to trip the springing man. Tom made a tackle but the Spaniard swerved. That swerve enabled Cliff to snatch away the letter. Like a shot Cliff stepped backward, turned and in several quick strides reached the cottage door. He swung it open, dashed in, slammed the door. The Spaniard, baffled, said something under his breath and paused.

Tom and Nicky promptly executed a backward movement that drew them up, side by side, before the door. Both aggressors stared and showed that they were baffled.

Cliff appeared at the sitting room window which he lifted.

"You just cool down until I see what is in this that you are so afraid to have me see," he exclaimed.

The Spaniard, however, seemed to have recovered. There were neighbors, perhaps some of them were watching. Whatever was to be done must be done at the instant. He muttered something to the Indian and made a spring toward the window. He caught the lower edge before Cliff could slam it down, gave Cliff a push. The young man stumbled back and caught his foot on a chair; he saved a backward fall only by supple contortion.

At the same time Nicky and Tom sprang from the door to catch the Spaniard but found their coat collars in the powerful grip of the copper colored one behind them. He swung them off their balance and started to run them toward the steps, backward, scratching, clawing, trying to break his hold.

As Cliff recovered himself, still clinging to his letter he saw the man scramble into the room. He made a fresh clutch at the envelope but Cliff sent it spinning into a corner, then felt powerful fingers grasp his arm.

At the same time a small automobile turned into the street. Nicky shouted, "Mr. Whitley!" as Tom, fighting ferociously, tore loose from his captor. He made a stroke but the Indian flung them both away at the top of the steps and vaulted the porch rail at one end with a shout as the car brakes screamed and the tires smoked. Before the car was at a standstill its occupant, his strong face set and intent, was coming with long strides up the path.

"Let him go," Tom called as the rescuer swerved to pursue the Indian. Tom saved Nicky a nasty fall down the steps and turned to see how Cliff was faring, shouting to the newcomer to come with him. Nicky, catching his equilibrium, went with them through the cottage door.

Within, Cliff was striving to hold back while his captor, who clung to Cliff as Cliff clung to him, pulled steadily and surely to where he could reach for the letter on the floor.

Cliff felt that he must act swiftly; he heard the noise on the porch but could not tell what had happened. He used a jui-jitsu trick taught him by a young Japanese student at Amadale, and the Spaniard, with a muttered word, crumpled for an instant; it was enough; Cliff had caught the letter and put the table between them by the time his adversary was up.

He was trapped; Cliff blocked the window; three were entering the door. Nevertheless, with a final, futile snatch at the object in Cliff's hand, the Spaniard caught up a chair and sent it sidewise against the legs of his advancing attackers; in their scuffle and scramble he avoided them, got to the door and was gone before they could right themselves.

"Don't chase him," Cliff panted. "Thank you for coming, Mr. Whitley. Everything is all right. They wanted this letter—but they did not get it!"

They all observed one another. Mr. Whitley was the youngest instructor at Amadale; he taught history and was a great friend of Cliff. His method of teaching made him popular with all the youths and boys at the Academy. His classes were more like round-a-camp-fire gatherings, with chats and anecdotes, than like cold, matter-of-fact history lessons. The boys all liked and respected Mr. John Whitley. He was hardly more than twenty-four and had a companionable manner and clear honest eyes. His sense of fairness made him mark examinations so justly that no student ever complained of favoritism.

"What is it all about?" he asked, "If that is any of my affair."

Cliff promptly began to tell about the arrival of the two men, their strange question followed by the coming of the letter.

And while he talked he began to make signs that were not noticeable to anyone who did not understand them. In actual fact his gestures were part of the secret signs of an order to which the three chums had pledged themselves. They could carry on communication that each understood but without giving away to others the secrets they discussed.

Thus, when Cliff scratched his ear with the middle finger of his left hand, he called for a secret council; when his chums folded their arms quietly it signified that they understood and that the lodge was convened.

Cliff talked to Mr. Whitley, told him everything up to the rescue. In the meanwhile he had appealed to his chums to judge the advisability of admitting Mr. Whitley to their secrets. Nicky, who was more excitable than Tom, forgot that they were carrying on their communication secretly.

"Make him take the oath—and—and everything!" he cried.

Naturally, unaware that they had decided to accept him, Mr. Whitley was surprised at Nicky's cry. Cliff explained.

"We have a secret order that we call The Mystery Boys!" he said, "we can talk together by signals so no one else understands. Each one of us has a mystery and that is why we formed the order. I don't know what became of my father, since he went to Peru, and Tom's sister has been missing for years, and Nicky has an old cipher in his family. These mysteries kind of drew us together and we formed ourselves into a band——"

"'The Mystery Boys!'" broke in Nicky.

"We have secret signs so that we can carry on a conversation right in front of you—as we just did while I told you some things," Cliff explained, "you see, Mr. Whitley, we have sworn not to tell our secrets to anyone who was not under the Oath of the Oracle——'by the sacred Emblem'," he quoted, "'Seeing All, I see nothing; Knowing All, I know nothing; Telling All, I tell nothing!'"

"I don't quite see," began the mystified instructor—what this has to do with the two men, he would have added, but Tom spoke up.

"We have decided that we need your help," he said, "we have talked it over together and we want you to know all about Cliff's mystery and advise us—but we can't break our oath."

"Oh! That clears it all up. Very well. I am willing to help Cliff, that is certain. If I have to promise things and join your order, I am willing. But can we not dispense with all but the promises just now and discover what is in that letter?"

"Let's!" urged Cliff, "I want to see what it is."

"Well——'On the Sacred Emblem'——" Mr. Whitley, who had a good memory, repeated the oath solemnly, his hand on a curiously cut Egyptian scarab, the sacred beetle of the ancient Egyptian mysteries which Cliff produced from among his father's collection in a cabinet.

"Now," he added, "let's see the letter, Cliff."

CHAPTER III
GOLD, AND A LIFE AT STAKE

Cliff was quite as anxious as the others to see what the envelope from Peru contained; he slit it and drew out two folded papers.

While the others watched eagerly he glanced hastily at one paper and crammed it into his pocket as he opened the second.

"It is!" he cried, "It is from my father!"

They crowded closer and urged him to read it aloud. The letter, after the address, fortunately placed there so that the destination was known even when its outer cover was spoiled in the river, was amazing.

"Dear Son and dear Lucy:

"If you ever receive this it will be fond love and farewell.

"I am in a city in the most inaccessible valley of the Andes. When the Spaniards conquered Peru some Incas and their subjects fled here and set up a city. I have tried for over four years to get away but there is no place where the cliffs can be climbed.

"When first I went to Quito I saved a native who was very ill. In gratitude he told me of this hidden city and even guided me to a mountain where a glimpse of it was possible; but he would not help me to enter the valley. When I said I must explore and study it he deserted me. Later I lowered myself with a rope and found a city of the old Inca sort, filled with gold."

"In the old Inca empire, before the Spanish looted it," Mr. Whitley broke in, "gold was so plentiful that it was used for dishes, utensils, ornaments, even for decorating their temples to the sun, which they worshipped as a god—but go on, Cliff."

Cliff finished the letter without further interruption.

"It is a perfect treasure land. But, though there is a way in, there is no way out. The natives are kind but they took away my rope; they do not want me to escape and bring the outside world to their hidden place.

"Being anxious to explain my absence I have trained and tamed a young eagle and I am fastening this to its leg in the remote chance that it may be found when I release him.

"If so, dear son Cliff—and sister Lucy—goodbye. I am very ill and fear I may not get better.

"Your loving "FATHER AND BROTHER."

"My!" exclaimed Nicky, "but people get well, Cliff," as he saw the depression in his chum's face.

"The Spaniard told a different story," Tom said, thoughtfully, "I think he wanted to get this for the Indian, to prevent you from learning where your father is. The Incas may be afraid you will try to go there."

"I would," Cliff said eagerly, "If——" ruefully "——I had any money and knew where it was."

"What was the other paper?" Mr. Whitley inquired.

Cliff had forgotten it; he drew it from his pocket and read it aloud. It was in the same handwriting that the envelope bore, and was in a style totally different from his father's letter.

Cliff, reading its clipped sentences slowly, began to tremble with excitement. When he finished and looked around he saw in the faces about him eagerness, hope, wistfulness.

The letter read:

"Clifford Gray; Sir:

"You don't know me. I don't know you. But I think we will know each other.

"I caught a tame eaglet and found your pa's letter. There was a map, too. It was to show how he got to where he went into the valley.

"I kept the map. Tell you why. I went to the place and saw the valley. I am a prospector and know these cordillerras.

"Reason I kept the map is I want to be with you if you go to find your pa. If you don't it's not any use to you anyhow. If you do I can help.

"What I want is some of that Inca gold. Not a lot. Enough to settle down, buy a ranch, live easy. I will be in Cuzco at the Tambo Atahualpa—that means Atahualpa hotel, for a while, till I hear from you. Let me know. With you and a couple more I could find your father and we could get him out.

"Signed respectfully, "QUIPU BILL SANDERS."

"Oh—if we could!" Cliff said. It was clear that his comrades felt exactly as he did.

Mr. Whitley was very thoughtful. While the trio discussed possibilities and re-read the two letters time after time, he sat without saying anything. Finally he looked up.

"See here," he told them, "you have made me a member of your secret order and asked for advice." They nodded eagerly.

"I think," he went on, "that if your relatives would let you go with me, it would be an instructive and an interesting trip."

The chums agreed with that quite heartily. But how?—where was money to come from?

"I have been given some money recently. I inherited it," Mr. Whitley informed them, "I will be glad to advance the amount for expenses. If we find Cliff's father and rescue him I shall feel that the money is well spent."

"And there is the treasure!" Nicky exclaimed.

"Yes," John Whitley agreed. There began an eager discussion of what they would do with their shares; but the young history instructor became rather serious.

"I am not so sure that we will try to get the treasure," he told them. Their faces fell, but they did not argue.

"You see," he went on, "we aren't going to be thieves. That treasure is the Incas' own; it isn't like buried gold. Of course, the people have taken a white man prisoner, and perhaps if we find it wise to take enough away from them to reimburse us for the expenses, it would not be dishonest."

"I agree with you," Cliff declared, "anyway, if we do find my father——" a hope which his chums eagerly echoed, "——he will be able to get all the royalties from his other books, which the publishers have held back, not knowing what to do, and only giving me enough to pay expenses. He will share with us all. My father is that kind of man!"

They were quite satisfied. The adventure would be sufficient as Tom put it.

Eager were their plans. Lists of things to take were made; plentiful discussions ensued, even amounting almost to arguments, for Nicky wanted a full arsenal of weapons, and enough ammunition to load down a mule. But he gave it up, for Cliff, from a study of his father's notes for part of his book, assured them that the Incas were not very warlike or cruel. They were not like the Mexican Aztecs, who, in days past, had been cruel and harsh. The

Incas, he said, were rather gentle, making war only in self defense, or to add territory when it was essential to their growth of empire.

Cliff, from his studies, conceived a great plan. Mr. Whitley agreed that it would be worth trying. What it was, and how it would work out, only time could tell; but it was so well thought of that some special articles were included in their supplies in order that they could use Cliff's method of entry into the country.

"Of course that means if you boys go beyond Cuzco with us," John Whitley said, when he had secured parents' consent to the adventure and had given promises to avoid danger. The chums felt very certain that they would go well beyond Cuzco, old Inca city, once capital of their vast empire.

In time goodbyes were said, final promises made, handkerchiefs waved from a departing train. The day spent in New York was a delight to the chums, and so was the embarkation on the great white fruit liner which would take them southward.

They laughed when, soon after the boat sailed, great clusters of bananas were placed within easy reach of passengers; that was a custom on the liners and it made the tropics seem very real and quite close already. The days of their voyage to the Panama Canal were spent in studying some books of Inca lore, and in working out better systems of signals for the Mystery Boys' order.

The passage through the Canal, the visit to one of its huge mechanically worked locks, the sights of the strange mingling of East and West in Panama City, added zest to the trip.

Then, tracing the route taken by the original Spanish caravels, they turned, as Nick said, "down the map," along the South American coast, and landed at Lima, in Peru, where Mr. Whitley wanted to locate an old acquaintance of his college days and get more information and a proper set of ancient Inca costumes, if possible, for use in Cliff's plan.

They found the city a thriving one and spent pleasant days there. The journey to Cuzco seemed almost endless, so eager were they. But, like all things that depend on time, the trip was eventually completed and the chums, hardly able to speak for their suppressed excitement, saw the first glimpses of what Cliff termed "The Gateway to Adventure"—Cuzco!

CHAPTER IV
"QUIPU BILL"

Romance! Adventure. To Cliff, Tom and Nicky the ancient capital city of the Inca empire was built on those two words.

Not that Cuzco, when they reached it, had any of its old treasures; Spanish invaders had stripped it centuries before. But the memory was there among the ruins.

The native Peruvian Indians—over whom the Incas had ruled, for the Incas were a superior tribe which governed its subjects kindly but firmly—these natives were shiftless, poor and inclined to be lazy.

But to the three adventurers, with their imaginations fired by what Cliff had read and what Mr. Whitley had told them on the boats, Cuzco still echoed to the tramp of armies carrying bows and arrows, swords and light shields; the great square shook again to the shouts of hosts gathered for ceremonies and feasting in the rites of their worship of the Sun.

"It is certainly interesting," declared Cliff, as they stood near the stripped temple which had once rivaled in splendor any other place of worship ever built. "The gold cornice is gone and so is the silver and so are the emeralds and ornaments. But we can imagine them. And notice how perfectly the edges of these stones are ground and fitted and matched."

"How big they are, too," Nicky added, "tons, some of them must weigh. The Incas had no beasts of burden to haul things—how they ever got these stones cut and shaped and hauled here and lifted into place—it is too much for me."

"Patience and time did it," Tom said, "I believe they say it took fifty thousand men twenty years and more to build one great palace or temple."

"With their hands—and without iron tools," Cliff added, "they mixed some tin with copper and made an alloy that they could make almost as hard as steel. But their roads and their aqueducts and their buildings all took labor and plenty of it."

"Isn't it time we started for the hotel?" Tom glanced at his watch, "Quipu Bill Sanders is to come to see us at four."

They agreed and turned to retrace their way around the ruin.

As they rounded a corner Cliff, in the lead, stopped sharply, in surprise. While there was one chance in a thousand that they should encounter the very Indian who had been with the Spaniard in Amadale, it was certain that the fellow into whom Cliff had almost banged had turned and seemed to stiffen when he saw them.

He stood facing a slender fellow, almost a boy, whose well developed leg muscles made Cliff think of a runner. With a swift word under his breath as the trio of chums stared, the Indian sent the youth off; and he was a runner and no mistake. He went lightly but with almost incredible speed down the road. The stalwart Indian paid no attention to Cliff but hastened away.

"Do you think he was——?" Nicky whispered.

"He jumped," Tom replied.

"Ought we to follow him?" Nicky wondered.

Cliff thought not. The runner was gone, the Indian might have been surprised to see white youths turn suddenly into view. Cliff could see no advantage to be gained by following.

They crossed the square to enter one of the four straight avenues which quartered the city. Cuzco was beautifully laid out, every ancient street as straight as if made by a surveyer's lines. Presently they reached the "tambo" or inn.

Bill Sanders was already there: he and John Whitley were in the courtyard around which all the rooms opened. Bill was squatted on his heels, cowboy fashion, with a knife in his hand, idly whittling a stick.

As he saw them and stood up they saw that he was tall and very thin; so thin, in fact, that he looked more like an underfed man than a tough, sinewy, sturdy mountaineer. However his skin was brown with healthy exposure and his grip, when they shook hands, made Nicky wince a little.

Quipu Bill Sanders had the eyes of a fox and the courage of a lion; and he was cunning, too; but his cunning was not the stealthy, wicked sort.

"You know who I am," he greeted. "Let's see if I know which of you is which."

Cliff, who had discovered a little skein of colored yarn at the roadside near the inn entrance and who had paused to glance at it and slip it aimlessly in his pocket as some decorative native object about which he would ask later, came forward at once.

"You're Cliff," said Bill. "The others stood back for you. And this is Tom—because he sort of fits his name, for he looks quiet and has a manly grip. Of course there's only Nicky left so this must be Nicky."

They smiled at his deduction and felt as though they had known him for a long time, he was so easy to meet. He already called Mr. Whitley by his first name, insisted they call him Bill, and alluded to them as "comrade" or "comrade Cliff."

"How is it you are called 'Quipu' Bill?" Nicky asked at once.

Bill squatted and began work on his stick again.

"The Incas didn't have any alphabet or writing to keep their records and history," Bill answered, "Nor any stone carvings such as you see in Egypt. When they wanted to send a message or make a record, or even figure up accounts, they used wool yarn of different colors and wove it together with different knots. The colors meant something and so did the placing of the knots and the number and the way they were made."

"They called these records or messages 'quipus' and a fellow who understood them, could make them and read them, was a 'quipucamayu.'"

"And you studied and got to be one of them," Nicky guessed.

"Yep! So I shortened it down to just the name of the yarn message."

"Were they like this? Isn't this one?" asked Cliff, recalling what he had found. He produced it. Bill nodded.

"That's one. Where did you get it?"

Cliff told him. Bill dropped his stick and became suddenly mighty serious.

"Why—look here! This is queer. This thing is a message about two grown men and some children and mountains and the snowy pass—and war—or ambush——"

He began to study the short woven length with its knotted strands and its weave of colors, some white, a bit of red and other colors mingled.

Then he looked up as he saw Tom's eyes turn toward the road, visible from the courtyard. They all looked. A youth—it might be the one they had seen before—was searching. He went along, head bent low, eyes on the road, turning from side to side.

Bill rose, dropping the quipu carelessly into his left coat pocket. Cliff, who was always observant, noted it though he paid little attention, being too busy wondering what Bill meant to do.

He went to the road and called. The youth turned, came back to him. There was a brief exchange of words, too far away to be heard. Then Bill put a hand in his pocket, drew out an object of woven yarn. The boyish fellow almost snatched it and while Bill called and pretended to be very angry the boy dashed out of sight and Bill strolled back to the party.

"For Pete's sake!" exclaimed Mr. Whitley, appearing exasperated. "You gave him that quipu."

"I gave him that quipu—yep."

"But—with the Spaniard visiting America to forestall that letter and with our lads seeing the Indian give that runner a quipu—don't you see that the message might have been about us?"

Bill nodded. "It all hooks up. It likely was," he agreed.

John Whitley stared, as did Nicky and Tom. Was this new acquaintance as much on their side as he claimed to be?

"Wasn't that the same boy you saw?" John Whitley inquired.

"It was, sir," Nicky answered. "He had a bright yellow thing-umjig on his head."

Bill whittled one side of his stick to satiny smoothness. "Now I don't know your mind and you don't know mine," he said, "But——"

"Wait!" broke in Cliff. "You dropped that quipu into your left hand pocket, Bill. I think—I'm sure—I saw you take what you gave him out of the other side of your coat."

Bill grinned approval. "Right as can be," he agreed. "I had picked up an old quipu in my diggings to show you fellows and that's the one I gave him." He showed them the other one, still where he had dropped it in his pocket. "He's taking—to whoever he's sent to find—a quipu that has a history or record of how a great sky god, or courtier of the Sun-god that they worship—of how this Chasca came to earth and brought great peace and prosperity to the Inca people."

"Why, that fits in with my plan!" exclaimed Cliff.

"So it does," said Mr. Whitley.

They had a long discussion. Bill told them that he "figured" that the Indian who had been with the Spaniard had been sent out from the hidden city to try and prevent the letter from being delivered.

"They must have learned about it," he said, "and guess they tried to stop it. Then, when they failed, they let us come on down here, where we are, in a way of speaking, right in their hands——"

"That means that Cuzco is as far as our young chums will go," said Mr. Whitley seriously. The youthful faces became downcast. "I promised not to take you into danger," continued their Captain, as Bill named him, "and so Cuzco will be your stopping place." There was no argument. The Captain's word was law.

But events were to compel a change in Mr. Whitley's ideas.

CHAPTER V
THE CHUMS SHOW THEIR METTLE

In Cuzco, while final plans were made and supplies were being assembled, the chums were free, for several days, to explore. Bill had shown them their map, which he had kept out of Mr. Grey's note when he coaxed the eaglet to his camp. The map did not mean much to them, but to Bill, who had already gone alone over the passes to be sure there was a hidden city, the map was quite clear. They would go on foot over the mountains, he said. It was safer than by muleback: some of the passes were quite narrow and dangerous, although he could show the best ones to them.

The chums were rather depressed that they could not accompany Mr. Whitley and Bill: however they agreed to make the best of it, and with the naturally buoyant spirits of youths in a new place they went about and had a fine time.

One of the people they met was a youth, quite near their own ages. He spoke a little English and acted as their guide.

None of them, nor their older companions, suspected his real purpose, but it was divulged, one day, as they were in a meaner quarter of the city where some of the natives of Peru, degraded and listless remains of a once noble race, had their poor homes.

"Come—here—I show—how I live!" said their young guide. They all followed him into a low room in an old building, squat and roughly built of a composition something like the *adobe* of the Mexicans.

But once they were inside they turned in dismay. The youth was not alone with them: three fierce looking half-caste men, part Inca, part Spanish, rose from a dark corner: one slammed the rude door and fastened it. "Now," he said, "you stay here."

"What's the big idea?" demanded Nicky hotly, relapsing into slang in his excitement.

"You see!" said the man. He and his companions held a low-voiced conference and then one of them rose and was gone: his malevolent looking friends gave the door a vicious slam and shot its bolt.

"What are you going to do with us?" demanded Tom.

"We keep you. When that tall one—" he meant Mr. Whitley,"—start for Lima once more, we let you go!"

"You daren't!" cried Nicky, and made a dash for the window. But Tom and Cliff restrained him.

"We'll have the police—or whatever they're got here!" Nicky said. He gave a shout. But one of the men advanced with a very threatening gesture.

"Keep quiet," Tom urged and Cliff added, "we're in a strange place." He counseled, "We have to keep our heads. We'll find a way out but not by making a disturbance. We don't know these men or this part of town: we don't know the customs they have. If we keep quiet they may let us go or relax their guard."

"But then our trip's ruined!" argued Nicky.

"Yes," said Cliff, morosely, "and my father is the worst sufferer if he is still alive. But we are trapped. We must do our best to get out of it before they send that man to Mr. Whitley."

"He's already gone," grumbled Nicky.

"No he isn't. He's just outside. I see him through the window. He's rolling a cigarette out there by a post."

"He's waiting for someone," said Tom, "I see him."

"Tom," whispered Nicky, "your uncle gave you a pistol, didn't he? Have you got it? Let's shoot our way out!"

That was Nicky all over! He was excitable and quick. He knew that Tom had been trusted to carry a light .22-caliber revolver given him by his uncle, because Tom had a cool head and would not abuse the possession. It was more for signalling, than for a fight.

"Easy, Nicky!" counseled Tom, "We don't want to hurt anybody."

"No," chimed in Cliff, "we're outnumbered and we don't know how dangerous this neighborhood may be. Besides, if we do anything to get into police courts it will make us tell what we are going to do and that will upset all Mr. Whitley's plans."

"They're upset already," Nicky grumbled, "That man's gone———"

"No he isn't," Tom replied, "He's waiting outside, by a post—I can see him through the window. There! Why—I believe the very same Indian we saw by the temple is giving him money!"

"Yes—I'm sure it's the same one," Cliff said, "He's coming in."

The tall Indian, or Inca noble, for he was really that, was admitted. The two waiting men stretched out eager hands.

"We get them," said one, "You pay. We go." Then he remembered that he spoke a half-halting English, and repeated it in dialect.

The Indian paid them some money and the two men, as if glad to be away, left quickly. The boy came in, acting shamefaced, but trying to look cheerful. He, too, stretched out a hand.

"Now—if only we had some way to take these two by surprise," began Tom.

"Sh-h-h!" warned Nicky, "They'll hear you."

Cliff reminded him that the Indian had not understood the half-breeds when one spoke in English, and that the boy had to stop and translate. He spoke in low, eager tones.

"Nicky, what did you do with that little box of magnesium powder you took out of the supplies this morning? You were going to try to take a daylight kodak picture inside a temple by flashlight. If you had it, now——"

"I have," Nicky whispered, "but——"

"Listen. Here's a plan. It may work. It would play on the superstitions of these fellows. They are both natives and I don't think either one has seen a flashlight, or an electric torch. If we could make them think we were powerful magicians and could burn them, they might be scared enough to be off guard——"

"It's an idea!" exulted Tom, "I have that small burning glass, Cliff—suppose I got to the window, and set the burning glass so it focuses, while the man is paying the boy. Then——" That was Cliff's idea, too. Tom moved quietly over and pretended to look out of the window. Really, he was adjusting a small lens, hidden by his hand on the stone window ledge, so it focused the sun rays in one spot. On Cliff's instructions Nicky maneuvered his body to help conceal the tiny lens from the sight of the others. Tom opened the flash powder box, a small, single charge of magnesium powder which, when ignited, makes a great white flash and a big puff of smoke, but is not dangerous.

The boy turned from being paid.

"Listen," Cliff commanded, "You—tell—that—man—" he spoke slowly and impressively, "—we—are—going—away—from—here. If—he—tries—to—stop—us, we—will—burn—him—up!"

The boy stared. Cliff repeated his words. The boy, mystified, translated. The man laughed scornfully. Cliff drew a small pocket electric flashlamp into view. In a dark corner he played the rays while the natives stared. Then, suddenly, he pointed a dramatic finger at the tiny box on the window ledge. The natives stared at it curiously, not knowing what to expect.

"Tell—him—we—burn—that—box—to—show—what   happen—to you—if—you—stop us!" Cliff said with a bold and threatening expression.

The boy spoke in dialect and both seemed unable to take their eyes off the box.

Cliff made a sign to Tom who pushed the small box into the focus of the lens which Nicky screened from the natives' view. Cliff pressed his light switch, and pointed the ray with a few signs of his free hand.

Nothing happened!

The man laughed and the boy snickered. Nicky began to feel weak and cold; but Cliff stood his ground.

Then, so suddenly as to startle even Nicky, the focused rays ignited the powder: there was a dull "boop!" and a blinding glare.

Before the smoke had risen and began to spread Cliff whispered, "Now— make for the door!"

Holding the flashlight pointed at the boy until the latter cowered back against the man, Cliff led his chums to the door. He fumbled with the catch: the man made a move as if to grapple with him but Cliff threw the ray into his eyes and he flung up his arm, instinctive fear of something not understood overcoming his wit. Cliff unfastened the clumsy catch, the chums fled to the street and were off like young gazelles.

"They'll find the lens!" Nicky panted.

"What do we care?" demanded Tom, "They won't get us!"

Of course all plans had to be altered; the youths could not be left behind. They were glad that in trying to prevent the expedition the Indian had only made their part in it certain.

On a fine evening, with all the natives engaged, and with all supplies packed, and with their course through the mountains carefully determined, they went to sleep for the last time in a civilized hotel—if the mean accommodations of the place they had selected could be called "civilized." Mr. Whitley's Lima friend had not proved a very good adviser. However, bright and early the next clear, temperate day—for Cuzco was not in the hotter lowlands where tropical heat was fiercest—they began their real adventure.

Bill and Mr. Whitley were in advance: then came the natives, laden with quite heavy packs, under which they toiled along on an ever ascending slope, singing native chants and talking in their unintelligible jargon. Behind them came the Mystery Boys, also laden with packs containing personal things and articles they wished to protect from prying eyes.

"We're on our way," they told each other and felt like capering at the certainty that in trying to frustrate their plans the Indian had made it possible for them to go along.

Up in the hills a tall, well built Indian stood with several companions, watching the lower passes.

One day, as the comrades toiled along, entering the real mountains, the vigilant watcher turned toward his companions.

"Brother, they come!" he said.

"They come—yes," agreed his nearest aide, a noble of the old and almost extinct true-blooded Incas, "They come—yes."

He made a meaning gesture.

"But—they will not come back!"

That same day Cliff borrowed Bill's field glasses and focused them on a small band, toiling along far behind them.

"I think we're being followed—I've noticed that group several times," he told the older members of their party.

They agreed, and frequently thereafter the followers were observed, but always too far behind to enable the chums to guess their identity. Was it the Spaniard? Was it the Indian?

Many days passed and they were well in the high cliffs before they learned the truth!

CHAPTER VI
A NEW MYSTERY DEVELOPS

Quichua, the almost universal dialect which the Incas had introduced into Peru as they conquered its tribes, was quite well understood by Bill Sanders. He spent much time on their daily marches, and in camp, teaching it to John Whitley and the three chums. It was the language that the hidden city's inhabitants would be most apt to understand, he believed.

When they had learned that a "chasqui" was a runner or messenger; that Cuzco, the name of the principal city and hub of the old empire was so called because the word meant navel, the center of the body; and many other things such as that "Pelu" meant river and was thought by some to have been the word that gave the Spaniards their name for the nation—Peru!—they began to study brief sentences and after a while could hold short and simple conversations together.

In return they taught Mr. Whitley and Bill the secret ways of exchanging ideas in the signals of their order. After some discussion and hesitation Bill was made a member of The Mystery Boys and although the chums debated the good sense of letting him know all their signs, they finally gave them to him—and as events proved, they were to be glad they had done so.

In camp Cliff and his friends spent a great deal of time studying the rude map: because Quipu Bill had some misgivings about letting the only guide they had become damaged or lost, Tom, who was quite a draftsman, made a very good copy which they used and over which they watched jealously so that the natives would not discover what it was.

The small party—not more than eight—which had been following them hung on like wolves on the flank of a buck: when Bill hurried along the others kept the same distance, when his party lagged the others dallied also.

"I think it is either the Indian, or the Spaniard, or both of them," said Bill, "They know—at least the Spaniard does—that there was a map, for he was in camp when I caught the eaglet." But the other party kept just too far behind for them to see, even with fine glasses, just who comprised the group.

Then, one afternoon, Cliff looked down from a high point and called to Bill.

"Bill—get out your field glasses. I don't see that party anywhere below." Bill looked. John Whitley and the youths took their turns. But there was no sign of pursuit.

"We must have lost them," Nicky said.

"But we have been on a straight road all day," Mr. Whitley objected. "No. Either they have dropped too far behind for us to see them at all, or they have given it up——"

"Or they have turned into some side pass, thinking that can get around us in some way," Bill added, "But they won't. I guess we have lost them for good."

They all felt rather glad of it. There had been some fun in the game of hare and hounds at first, but after a few days the continual watching became wearisome and perhaps worrisome. Their natives noticed it, for one thing, and they did not want the Peruvians to think their story of an engineering and educational trip was a ruse. They all breathed more freely that night as they made camp.

But Cliff kept wondering why the pursuit had stopped.

That night—and it was cold for they were very high up in the levels just a little below snow level—he lay rolled in his blanket, in the tent the chums shared, thinking about it.

"Cliff," Tom's voice whispered through the dark, "Are you asleep?"

"No," Cliff answered under his breath. But he need not have been so cautious. Nicky was not asleep, either: and he declared the fact promptly.

"I'm awake too. Is it to be a session of the Inner Circle?"

"Maybe," Tom replied, "I was going to ask Cliff if he noticed that Indian that Bill calls Whackey—the one whose name is Huayca?"

"Notice him? Notice what about him?" Nicky demanded.

"He kept dropping back from one carrier to the next one, right along the line, today."

"Yes," Cliff said, "I saw him. He talked to each one for a few minutes, then he dropped behind and talked to the next one."

"What do you suppose it meant?" Nicky wondered. "Nothing, I guess. I have seen him do it before."

"You have?" Cliff and Tom asked it at one instant.

"Certainly. But he is the boss isn't he? He has to give orders."

"When he gives orders he yells them out so that we all hear him," Tom objected.

"In the morning," Cliff said, "Let's ask Mr. Whitley and Bill if they have noticed." They agreed and discussed the curious disappearance of the trailing party for a while.

Then, suddenly, Cliff hissed under his breath, "Sh-h-h-h!"

They became alert, intent: they listened with straining ears.

"It was only some pebbles—a little landslide," Nicky whispered. "They do that in the mountains. I saw some pebbles slip this afternoon."

Nevertheless Cliff gently crawled out of his blanket and his head came in rather vigorous contact with Tom's cranium for he was doing the same thing. They forgot the bump in the excitement for more pebbles were clattering at a little distance.

Cliff and Tom unhooked their tent flap and without widening its opening much, looked into the dim, starlit night.

Nicky pushed his face between them. Each felt that the others were tense, Nicky was trembling a little. They stared and listened.

From a greater distance came the crackle of a broken twig.

Without a word Cliff pushed into the open and stared around. Then he saw figures, silent, drifting like spectres through the night, shadows with lumpy heads.

At first he almost cried out at a touch on his arm but in the instant that he controlled his impulse he realized that it came from Nicky's grip on his arm.

"It's Indians!" Nicky gasped.

"Yes," said Tom, at his side; then he added in a puzzled way, "But they are going away from us."

"It's our Indians———" Cliff said, "They're running away. Hey!" he shouted, then, poised to race after them, he called to his comrades to waken Bill and Mr. Whitley; but they were already awake and emerging dazedly from their tent as Cliff thrust the ground behind him with racing feet, in hot pursuit of figures now making no effort to be quiet as they galloped away.

It was a hazardous pursuit in the dark and on a strange mountain path; but Cliff had observed, as was his habit, while they climbed earlier in the day: he knew when to swerve to avoid a heavy boulder, he seemed to avoid by instinct the more pebbled and slippery parts.

While Nicky and Tom, after shouting the news, pounded in pursuit he overtook the hindmost runner.

"Stop—you!" he shouted. The man swerved. Cliff made a tackle. The man tripped, was down. Instantly Cliff was erect again and racing on while Tom caught up with the man already scrambling to his feet and held him until Nicky arrived.

Then, from behind them, Bill, in the dialect, yelled a call to halt to the natives. Cliff reached his second man and put a hand on his arm. From behind came the flash of Quipu Bill's rifle, fired into the air over the runners' heads.

They stopped, uncertainly, and Cliff, racing down the path, took advantage of the interval to get to a point where he could at least try to "bluff" and hold the men.

The natives clustered in a little knot. They had bundles on their heads—probably most of the camp food and supplies. Cliff shouted to them to stand while Mr. Whitley and Bill made a scrambling, awkward, but rapid approach.

"Running out at night with our grub, eh?" Bill snapped, "You *hombres* about face and back to camp!" He translated into dialect and they sullenly obeyed for he still carried his rifle.

"All of 'em here?" he asked Mr. Whitley, "it's so dark——"

"The fellow you call Whackey isn't!" Cliff cried. Then a queer misgiving assailed him. He rushed to Bill and whispered. Bill, bent to hear, stiffened.

"Glory-gosh!" he gasped, "Go and see. In my coat pocket!"

They herded their morose captives back to camp while Cliff made his hasty retreat and a thorough but equally hurried examination in certain places.

He met Bill, approaching anxiously with John Whitley.

"It's gone—the map's gone!" he gasped.

"So that's why the other party stopped following. That's why Whackey isn't around!" exclaimed the chief of the party.

"I saw him, today," Nicky cried, and explained, "Tom did, too."

"Planned to cut away during the night," Bill snapped, "Guess he planned deeper, too: I think he expected these natives to make enough noise to be caught—that gave him a chance to get the map. I wondered why he watched me so closely, last couple of days."

"Well, never mind," Mr. Whitley counseled, "He and the others he went to join cannot get there ahead of us. Bill knows the passes."

"All but one place after we get back to the snowy pass," Bill objected, "Cliff's pa only drew it rough and indicated the one right way—the way he took; but I know there's a regular slather of cross cuts and paths between the cliffs up there. It's all torn up by some earthquake long ago. I'd need the map there!"

"Well, we have the copy Tom made——" but Mr. Whitley stopped, arrested by Cliff's clutch on his arm. Flashlights trained, the five, with a solemn warning to the natives, who seemed not to know what to do and so were for the time in no danger of mischief, hurried into Cliff's tent. They flicked their lights around but Cliff, catching one from Nicky, trained it on the ground cloth.

Tiny fragments of paper, too fine ever to match together, littered the cloth under Tom's little writing case!

CHAPTER VII
CLIFF TRIES A RUSE

When Quipu Bill questioned the Peruvians they remained sullenly wordless. What he called the vanished Whackey was, fortunately, expressed in Spanish; otherwise it would have called for reproof from Mr. Whitley.

"What are you going to do?" John Whitley asked as Bill threw a fresh shell into the magazine of his rifle and offered the weapon to him.

"You stand guard till dawn," Bill replied, "Don't let one of these *hombres* leave. The rifle is only to scare them—I don't expect you to use it. I'm going after that Whackey and get that map back."

Tom, who had been very thoughtful, spoke up.

"Are you certain that you can trail him?" he asked.

Bill grinned in the light of their rekindled campfire. "He may go a roundabout way," he stated, "But he is bound to end up at the Spaniard's camp. That's where I'll go. I can locate it. That party must be somewhere behind us, maybe in a cut that's out of sight of the main pass."

"What Tom is thinking is that it might not be the Spaniard's party, I believe," Cliff said. Tom nodded.

"There is the man—or the men—that runner was sent to find," Tom suggested.

"That is so," said Mr. Whitley, "How can you know which party is behind this affair?"

"I don't," Bill admitted, "But the Spaniard's crowd stopped dogging us just before this happened."

"Perhaps his natives have started trouble—or deserted," Mr. Whitley hinted.

"I think the Spaniard would have told Whackey to take both maps," Nicky said, "It would take less time to grab a paper than to stand and tear it to pieces."

"Maybe Whackey did that on his own inspiration," Bill said.

"Then the evidence points more toward the Incas than toward the Spaniard," Cliff urged, "The Spaniard is cunning enough not to leave anything to be decided by Whackey."

Bill began to whittle on a stick, thinking. He nodded.

"You may be right," he agreed, "We must find out which party has the map. If it is the Spaniard we can hide and let him pass and then trail him; but if it is the other side, then we must either take a long chance at finding the one right path or else we must give up the trip."

Cliff thought of his father. Perhaps he was still alive; unless they completed their plans he might never know.

"Probably we will have to give up," said Mr. Whitley, "There are so many menacing things: I promised the relatives of our younger members———"

"We can at least be sure which side has the map," said Cliff, "Before we do give up."

"How can we find out?" asked Nicky eagerly.

Cliff explained a plan he had worked out. It was very simple, so simple that Bill poked fun at himself because he had not worked it out himself. He agreed, as did Mr. Whitley, that it was worth trying.

Carrying out the scheme, Bill called the natives.

"You tried to run away," he told them, "We don't want you now. We cannot trust you. Take food enough to get to your homes, or at least enough to get out of the mountains. And go."

To their surprise the natives protested.

"Not so," said the spokesman, "We not try run away. We do all to make you follow us while Huayca do what he plan."

"What did he plan?"

"That we not know. We must do that way. That all we know."

"I see the scheme, I think," Mr. Whitley told Bill, "Huayca made the natives pretend to be stealing the food, so that our attention would be concentrated on them while he took the map. It does not seem logical to me that natives as clever as these would make enough noise to attract attention otherwise."

"We not like to run away. You not pay us yet," said a native.

So they knew no more than before. But Cliff was not discouraged. "Now we must try the second part of my plan," he pleaded. Mr. Whitley sanctioned it, cautioning the youths to take no needless chances in the event of possible trouble. He remained with Bill's rifle, out of the direct glow of the fire, his eyes watchful, although the natives seemed content to lie down for sleep.

Cliff, Nicky, Tom and Bill made final plans and then drifted quietly away from camp, down the mountain pass.

"He has had time to get there—Whackey has," Tom whispered.

Bill agreed and no further conversation was used. For hours they moved like flitting ghosts, avoiding noise as much as they could.

In time Bill held out an arm against which, in turn, they came to a stop. He pointed to a very faint flicker that showed on a rock at the mouth of a narrow diverging break in the cliff. For an instant the flare of a bit of wood showed, then it died.

Its brief reflection on the rock showed them the location within the cleft of the hidden company: at least, it proved that someone was there with a fire; the deduction that followed was almost sure to be right. No one else was likely to be there.

When Bill came back, after a long silence, he had made a scouting trip into the cleft and in a whisper reported to the trio of chums that the camp was there. Final plans were made and Bill crept away again. Cliff held his radium dialed watch so that all three could watch the slow minutes crawl away.

It became a matter of seconds before they could act. And how the seconds dragged! But finally the hands touched an agreed point. "Now!" said Cliff.

They gathered hands full of pebbles and moved into the mouth of the cleft which they had not dared enter before for fear of making some noise that would disturb the camp. Now noise was their very purpose!

All together, at Cliff's word, as they saw the dull embers of the dying campfire, sole proof of the camp's existence, they shouted wildly, with all their lungs. At the same time there was a shower of pebbles, thrown wildly but toward and beyond the fire. Then they rushed closer, screeching, yelling, howling.

Excited, frightened cries greeted the surprise attack.

Then, like a beam of white fire, the flare of Bill's flashlight cut into the opened flap of a tent, the only one in camp. Guttural, surprised Spanish came from within.

Running feet and terrified cries proved that the surprise had demoralized the natives and put them to flight. But hardly had the flash cut into the darkness than it was out and Cliff, seeing it disappear, urged his comrades to retreat with him; their purpose was accomplished and they must be gone before the Spaniard could organize pursuit.

"I found him sound asleep when I threw the light on him," Bill said as they hurried back up the pass. "He was so dazzled by the light I know he didn't recognize me, with all the noise to muddle up his mind."

"Then he has no map," Cliff declared. "When he is surprised and can't take time to exercise his willpower a man does things by instinct; I read a lot about that in a book. If a man has something very valuable and he thinks—or doesn't have time to think—there is any sudden threat to its safety, he makes a grab for it."

"Well," Bill told them, "Our 'friend' Sancho Pizzara, was sound asleep and when I woke him up, with noise and excitement, he reached for his Crucifix. So, you see, he did not have the map stolen—unless Whackey failed to get there."

"This Sancho man would be awake—waiting," Tom objected.

"With his gun ready and—and everything!" Nicky added.

When they reported to Mr. Whitley he agreed that they had fixed the theft of the map and its destination. The Incas!

"That ends our trip," he declared, "I cannot risk our lads in such dangerous affairs."

Cliff did not argue; that was not his nature. He did not remind Mr. Whitley that the plan suggested by Cliff before they started and for which certain materials had been packed, would not be likely to incur any danger. He simply sat still and watched Nicky and Tom show their disappointment.

But when the camp was once more quiet, if not asleep, he spoke to his comrades quietly and later on slipped away.

CHAPTER VIII
THE OUTCOME

What Cliff planned to do was based more on intuition than on any carefully thought out ideas. When the excitement broke out it was early morning; by the time that the camp settled down again it was almost time for dawn. As he returned to his tent with Tom and Nicky he had a sudden flash of inspiration and when he saw that in spite of their excitement his two companions fell into futile speculation, he decided that what he wanted to do could be done only if he acted alone and at once. Discussion would only waste time; no one else could accompany him. Of course he thought of consulting his elders; but like any young fellow who had what appeared to be a bright idea he wanted to accomplish his plan alone and not have to turn it over to someone else.

So Cliff slipped quietly out of camp as the first pale gray of approaching daylight threw the peaks ahead into jagged silhouette.

They had already gone down the pass; that way they had failed. Cliff turned upward. He moved quickly, alertly, progressing rapidly.

His intuition had told him that it was probable that the Indian, Huayca, if he really did mean to go to the Incas, would want to be able to report to them what the white people did when their map was stolen.

That meant to Cliff that Huayca would only go far enough ahead to find a secure hiding place. He would not want to travel off into the next stretch of pass, which was very close to a deeply cut ravine, without daylight. He could hide and watch! He might!

"If I had to watch," Cliff thought, "I would find a place high up and out of sight. Not a tree, because I might be seen in a tree; but I would get up on a ledge if I could find one."

There were plenty of ledges because that part of the pass led through fissures broken in the mountain by some great force of Nature in past ages. But the problem was to locate the right and most probable one in the dark and then to ascend to its top.

Far above, toward the East, the sky began to glow with the first proof that the sun was stoking his fires for a new day; in the pass night still fought to hold its own. The light gave the higher points a greater prominence and helped Cliff while the darkness around him also helped him by hiding his moving form.

"From the shape of that ledge ahead," he said to himself, "I am coming to a bend in the pass; now that would be a fine spot if——"

He reached the bend; carefully he peered around. There ended the fissures; the pass, which had run between high cliffs, swung rather sharply around the nose of a ledge and ran along the side of an open depth, a valley filled with mist; in the dark Cliff could not tell how deep it was, nor how wide.

The ledge, right at the turn, projecting a trifle, and about sixty feet above his head, was an ideal spot to spy from; if he could find a way up it would give him a place to see the pass toward the camp and also around the bend.

"Such a ledge as that would be perfect for an ambush," he thought. Cliff had read how the Incas, in their battles against the invading Spaniards, had ambushed soldiers in these mountain passes, dropping rocks from points above them, loosing flights of arrows, stunning them with stones from the slings with which they were expert. Here was the spot for such an attack.

How did the Incas get to such ledges? As he remembered his history, Cliff thought of a ladder woven of osier strands, tough vines that were to be found in that country. Bridges were swung across mountain streams with twisted ropes and cables of those stout vines; with planks supported by them footways were made that swayed dizzily, dipped in terrifying fashion, but that gave safe crossings to sure footed mountaineers.

He stepped off the rocky path into brush under the lip of the ledge and, almost as much by feeling as by sight, explored the side of the cliff. There was nothing, at first, to reward his search; but after some time, cleverly hidden among the brush, he found twisted, sturdy ropes that were so woven as to give the shape of a rude ladder with sagging but staunch crosspieces of the same vines. The ladder ran upward as high as his arms could reach, and without any hesitation Cliff began to climb.

From its location his ladder could not be seen until one got well around the bend and there, for the light was better and he could see, the pass ran only a short way, then swung across one of those osier bridges, still kept in repair because this was one of the main-traveled paths. Amid the brush and stuff and with trees between it and the path, the ladder was not apt to attract attention. Its withes felt pliant and fresh with sap. Cliff decided that it was not an old ladder, but a new one, recently placed; perhaps for the very purpose to which Huayca might recently have put it.

As he neared the top, Cliff became cautious. He lifted himself slowly so that he would make very little noise. When his head was level with the top of the ledge he protruded it upward with utmost care and spied around, his eyes just able to see.

The flat top of the ledge, he saw, was about an acre in extent. It sloped slightly upward to the next sharp rise at the back and light showing from the brightening sky indicated a fissure, possibly another pass, in the cleft.

But his attention focused on a clump or mass of stone, quite large, near the middle of the level space.

In the pale light it bulked like a ghostly ruin. Cliff eased carefully until he could get to the *pajonal*—short, yellow grass of the mountains—which covered the top of that ledge.

Then he made his way with as soft a tread as he could, to the ruin. It looked as though, in some ancient day, a granary or rest house or barracks had been built; time had helped the frost and heat to crumble many of its stones, so that it had little shape; but at one point there seemed to be a rude hut rebuilt from the stones. Toward this Cliff crept.

He had scarcely reached the side of the small stone pile when he heard what at first sounded like a groan, but then was more like a yawn.

"Huayca!—I guess!" Cliff reasoned, "he came here and when he saw our fire die down—he could, from that further ledge—he decided to take a nap."

He wasted no time in hesitation while he thought; he sent his eyes darting here and there till he saw, close to the hut, a spot in the crumbled masonry where he could creep into a niche and be out of sight of anyone emerging from the hut door.

He squeezed into his niche only just in time. Yawning, stretching, a tall figure, arms flung wide, stood in the hut doorway for a moment, then strolled over toward the edge of the cliff, lay flat and peered toward Cliff's camp.

Cliff, peering from his hiding place, watched steadily. The Indian, for the light was strong enough to distinguish him as dark, lithe and dressed as a native, rose to a kneeling posture.

He fidgeted with his garments while Cliff became very intent. He saw the Indian draw a paper into view. He flattened it on his knee, and in the growing brightness studied it. Then, after an instant of hesitation, he drew off one of his sandal-like foot coverings and thrust the paper, folded, into the shoe.

Cliff did some hard thinking. This must be Huayca although the light did not yet give proof of that. But the paper did. Cliff's problem was this: if he disclosed his presence and tried to surprise the Indian the latter might escape—perhaps run to the fissure in the rocks and vanish. With the map—as Cliff surmised the paper must be—in his sandal it was imperative to capture him, and in such a way that Cliff could then be certain he would not destroy the map before Cliff could get it or summon help.

Therefore, his thinking made him determine that he must get the native into some situation where surprise and location would make up for Cliff's inferior strength and size.

He reasoned that no native would travel in the mountains without food. Therefore there must be some sort of pack within the hut; probably a pack containing some *charqui*—the dried, thin sliced deer meat which was a large part of a mountaineer's food, and dried or parched grain.

The Indian was again peering intently toward camp. Perhaps the fire was being made up by natives, or some other activity went forward. Cliff took the chance that the watcher would be so absorbed that he would not see a moving figure in the shadow beside the ruins.

Sidling along, stepping cautiously to avoid loose stones—for the least sound, in that stillness, would carry to keen Indian ears!—he slipped to the hut door and vanished inside it.

The place had no windows. Except for the doorway, lacking any door, there was no place where light could enter; since that opening faced the west, the interior was dark—pitch dark!

Cliff felt his way carefully. His foot touched something; he paused and stooped. Exploring fingers assured him that he had found a small pack; around it was a packstrap with some rope attached so that the pack could be tied up.

Loosening the rope, Cliff drew it free; with it he slipped back to the doorway and stopped just inside and beyond the dull glimmer of light it admitted. He saw the Indian fasten his sandal, rise and saunter toward the hut—for his breakfast.

Totally unsuspicious the Indian approached; Cliff held his breath. As the other stepped in Cliff's foot shot across the entry and the Indian, with no way to foresee the ruse, stumbled and fell forward. At the same instant Cliff moved.

With pantherish quickness he grasped the two feet which had flung out as the man fell; around them, before the other knew just what had attacked him, Cliff flung the rope, drawing taut the end; a slip-noose, cleverly maneuvered over the ankles, drew tight.

Then began a battle between the man, prone but able to kick and scramble, and Cliff, working to get his rope over a rock.

In the camp Mr. Whitley came from his tent, yawning; he had secured but a little sleep. He saw Tom and Nicky, beside the campfire and approached.

"Where is Cliff?"

"He went after Whackey before dawn." Bill, hearing, ran over.

"Why didn't he tell me?" Quipu Bill said in an injured voice, "I'm going after him. That Indian—if Cliff comes up with him at all—may be dangerous!"

"Look!" Nicky fairly screamed, "up there———"

His pointing finger called for no further words. They all turned their eyes up the pass. Outlined against the yellow and crimson of sunrise was a silhouetted figure, prancing.

Faintly came a shouted call.

Like racers at the clang of a bell the four were away up that pass. As they neared they heard Cliff calling down to them and telling about the ladder.

In the hut doorway they soon discovered a scowling but silent captive.

It was Huayca, without any mistake.

"How did you ever?———" began Mr. Whitley and Nicky, almost together.

Cliff explained. When he reached the point where he had the rope twisted about Huayca's ankles he grinned.

"He wriggled and yelled and squirmed," he said, "but I knew if I could keep his feet in the air long enough and didn't tire out first I would win; when he stopped wriggling I got a chance to pull home a slip-knot I made and then I got the rope end over that place in the stone—it was sort of like a pulley and when I hauled on the rope his feet were up in the air and I tied the rope and ran to call you."

"I wonder if he had the map?" Tom said.

Cliff walked to the man lying with his heels higher than his head, and jerked off a sandal.

Then they did slap Cliff's back!

CHAPTER IX
AMBUSHED!

What to do next was a problem. They discussed it, breakfasting after Huayca had been returned to camp. They had the map again; but, at the same time, they had native carriers who had tried to slip away under cover of darkness; they had Huayca, morose, sullen, who must be guarded constantly or released to slip away and tell the Incas of their movements.

The mystery of the Spaniard was cleared up: when Bill had gone to his camp the night before he had seen from the way the man stumbled up that his ankle had been turned; they had stopped to let it rest or to improvise a rude *hamaca*—the native sedan-chair or palanquin, really more of a stretcher.

They discussed matters from every angle but could not find a plan that suited them all. If they went ahead their natives might disappear with the very things that were most necessary to their plans: if they kept a guard it would show that they were not the innocent travellers that they claimed they were. Of course Huayca knew the truth; but had he told the other natives? If they went on he might make their carriers turn against him. If they released him he would certainly go straight to the Incas, perhaps leaving the natives prepared to desert them or to lead them into some trap and there desert them.

Their discussion had reached no end when they saw four natives coming up the pass, carrying a roughly made litter. In it was Pizzara, the Spaniard.

"I twis' the foot," he said after he had been brought to their circle and his litter had been set down. "Thank you very much, I have eat the breakfast."

He rolled a cigarette and they watched him without speech.

"You no fools," he declared, finally, "you know why I follow. When I was in Senor Sander's camp one Indian come and say he pay me for go to stop letter. I try but—" he nodded at Mr. Whitley, "—I not so lucky.

"But Indian disappear in Lima. He not pay me. So I think to follow you and so come to place where is much gold.

"But why must I follow? Let us join together. That way we are stronger."

They exchanged surprised glances.

At a slight shake of the head from Mr. Whitley, Bill spoke. They were not going after gold, he denied, they were going to try to rescue a white man held captive by Incas. They all knew, of course, Cliff thought, that it was useless to try to hoodwink the Spaniard: he knew all but the exact route. It was wiser to admit the truth.

"We will discuss your offer," John Whitley said, "perhaps we may agree to it. We will let you know later."

The Spaniard nodded, signaled to his bearers to remove his litter but instead of returning down the pass he was carried the other way. They saw why at once. His camp had been broken up and his natives, not very heavily loaded, for he traveled light, came up the path and overtook their master.

"I don't know how you feel and you don't know how I feel," Bill was whittling industriously as he spoke, "but it looks to me as though he has shown us the way out."

"I don't see how," Nicky broke in, "if we go with him he may spoil our plans and get the gold—and—and—everything!"

"He'd follow us, anyhow," Tom said.

"He won't make as much trouble if he is with us as he might the other way," Cliff agreed, "he could be watched."

"If his natives could carry some of our things," Mr. Whitley said, "we could discharge our own: they have not proved trustworthy."

"That is my idea," Bill nodded, "he has more muscle in his carriers than he is using. Shall we join forces?"

They decided to travel in company. The spokesman was Bill. He explained to Senor Pizzara that their own bearers had tried to run away with their supplies; if he would let his carriers take heavier loads so they could discharge their own, they would agree to his plan. He was eager to accept the proviso.

Over the swaying bridge of osier and plank that spanned a chasm they passed as one party; their own men went the other way with just enough food to last until they reached the foothills.

Huayca they kept with them. He was not openly guarded but either Bill or Mr. Whitley kept watch at night and he made no effort to escape.

Pizzara asked to see the map; there was no reason to refuse. He promised solemnly that he would help them in their effort to rescue Cliff's father if he still lived; he would provide one more to aid their plans, although these did not confide to him during the journey.

Up, ever up they toiled. Great cliffs of granite and porphyry, massive and awe-inspiring, lined the path. Vast chasms yawned beside the way. As Cliff expressed it, they were pygmies going through Nature's giant workshops, where heat and frost, sun and rain, earthquake and volcanic upheaval, tore apart what had been built and threw the odds and ends everywhere.

Colder and colder grew the sharp winds as they climbed into the snowy land above the timberline.

It was to such a scene of grand and wild awesomeness that the three chums turned smarting eyes, one icy morning, as they emerged from their tent.

Beyond their camp a great pair of twin peaks reared snowy crests into the golden light of dawn. Through the dip between those peaks ran the snowy pass marked in the map. They could see part of it already, from their camp in the slightly depressed space they had chosen in which to avoid as much wind sweep as possible. It was a gorgeous sight. Jagged rock, glistening white blankets of virgin snow, fire-lit at the peaks by the approaching sunbeams, deep clefts diving into pitchy darkness, made a sight they could never forget.

"But look!" said Nicky, first to get his fill of Nature's marvels, "There aren't any Indians!"

"Good gravy!" agreed Tom with his favorite exclamation. "You're right. Where—? Oh, Bill! Say, Bill!" He and the others raced toward the figure sitting composedly by a roaring dry-alcohol stove over whose wind-fanned blaze he was heating coffee. Mr. Whitley emerged from his tent, shivering, and joined them.

"What has happened?" he inquired.

"Just what I expected," Bill said. "The gay Spanish Don has taken his natives and gone on alone."

"Deserted us!" cried Mr. Whitley.

"Deserted his first love for gold!" grinned Bill. "Yep! I guessed he would, just about here."

The chums looked at him in dismay.

"Oh, he left all our supplies," Bill assured them. "Everything is intact. That's why I let him go."

"But what shall we do?" asked Nicky.

"Follow!" stated Tom.

"Not exactly," Bill corrected. "See—" he pointed toward the saddle-like depression between the peaks,—"he goes that way. We turn right around on our tracks and go back—that way!"

"Give up?" said Cliff, disappointedly.

"Nope! Climb down!"

They stared at him. Was good old Bill growing queer or was he trying to be funny?

"Climb down?" Nicky demanded. "Where? Why? And where is Whackey?"

"You don't know my mind, and—I'm not going to tell you!" Bill varied his usual formula. "As for Whackey, I let him go in the deep, dark night. We don't need him any more."

It was all a puzzle and baffled the young fellows. Mr. Whitley seemed to be deeper in Bill's confidence, for he smiled at them.

"Bill should not tease, up here in this cold place," he said. "The truth is, we are in the little cup of what must have been a high mountain lake. It is just low enough in altitude to be below the eternal ice line in summer. At present we are really camped on a vast cake of ice which has frozen over it since the past summer. It will stay this way until next year; then the ice will melt gradually and any snow that turns to water will add to the reservoir."

In centuries long gone, he explained, the Incas must have chosen this as one of their water-reservoir links. They had wonderfully perfect systems of aqueducts as the chums knew.

"At any rate," he proceeded, "Bill is engineer enough to surmise that the ruined and blocked-up stone depression we saw half a mile away is part of an old Inca 'pipe line' or aqueduct, and that this one communicates with others. In fact, when he came here the first time he saw that it was possible to pretend to give up and retrace our way, and then to dive into a sort of stone subway and go around to come out beyond the place where there might be an ambush."

"But the others will be caught," Cliff said, in dismay.

"I warned Pizzara several days ago that the Incas were watching for us," Bill declared. "He thought I was trying to frighten him. We can't chase him! I think the worst that can happen will be that the Incas will drive him back."

Which, in fact, was a good guess.

A week later, after they had plunged into a rock-buttressed cut and explored its communicating cuts, always working by compass to pass around the frozen lake, they came to a place where Bill halted them while he climbed the jagged, crumbled side of their cut to spy out the lay of the land.

It had been no fun, that week in the cut. Packs were all exceedingly heavy since five had to carry the loads of ten, even though depleted by weeks of travel during which the food had dwindled rapidly. So they struggled over rock debris, up sloping walls, over obstacles, sometimes in dark tunnels for a short distance; but as Bill returned to them they knew that it had been an effort well repaid.

"Trampled snow," he said. "Abandoned packs. Signs of a fight. Rocks dropped. Arrows stuck in the snow. I guess they turned our Spanish friend back, and turned him quick!"

Perhaps Bill did not tell quite all he had seen; nor did the boys press him for details.

Bill and Mr. Whitley decided that it was safe to go on; there were no signs of Indians. It was supposed that Huayca had joined his own forces; no doubt, seeing the white party turn and retrace its steps, he and the others decided that they had turned back; at any rate they were not to be seen, those Incas, though a sharp lookout was maintained.

Many were the adventures through which the chums passed; once, in the White Pass, the whole party lost its footing when Tom slipped and dragged them all over the edge of a small crevice in the ice; but the mountain climber's staff, which Bill had swiftly jammed in the ice, held them until they could scramble up—and the steep drop where the crevice widened just beyond was avoided.

Nicky found a wounded vicuna and tried to take the frightened little mountain sheep with them, but it disappeared during the night and they never knew whether one of the Andean eagles, of which they saw many, had swept it away or if in its struggles against its tether it had lost its footing and fallen over a precipice near the camp. Entering a cave to shelter for the night, they once surprised some of the huge vultures, having a feast on some frozen animal—Cliff and Nicky were badly buffeted by their wings in an effort to escape from the cave without rolling down a steep slide; but in time the high places were behind them and they began to drop slowly down into the verdure of the less chilly slopes.

After days of rest and other days of travel, they found themselves close to a wide valley, into which there seemed to be no entrance.

They were on a cliff, quite sheer in its drop to the vale beneath; but as they stared, Nicky lifted a hand and pointed—"Look!"

Far away they saw the hidden city!

CHAPTER X
THE HIDDEN CITY

"There it is," Nicky repeated, "There's—"

"Incaville?" suggested Tom, smiling.

"No—wait! I know! Quichaka!"

"Quichaka it is," said Bill. "But don't make any noise. If anybody is down below we don't want them to know about us until all our plans are completed."

They grew quiet, then, looking down for several hundred feet into the valley. To the right and to the left, similar cliffs and steep drops made the valley inaccessible. It had been well chosen as a retreat by the old tribe when the Spaniards came into their country; and it was not alone a safe retreat; it was a fertile valley also. Corn could be seen in great, green fields, and other spots were tilled and showed the bright colors of growing plants.

"The city is too far away to tell much about it, even with the field glasses," said Mr. Whitley. "But it is guarded by mountains even more rugged than those we have just passed through. We shall soon be in its streets, if all goes well."

They began to prepare at once for their descent into the valley.

It was their purpose to go in disguise. They had the clothing for their disguises and had carefully brought some herbs from which Bill had made a dye. They located a fairly deep depression in a rock, discovered a stream and carried their buckets full of water from it to the stone, a wilderness bathtub, as Cliff called it.

Nicky and Tom, just to be perverse, as an outlet for their enthusiasm, now that the real adventure was so near, declared: "It's a small depression in the rocks, selected by Bill!" Joking so, they created a small pool, large enough for their purposes.

Into the water Bill emptied a preparation he had guarded carefully from moisture and damage; it was a dye known to him, that turned the water a dull, murky mud color at first; but when it cleared, it made a limpid, brown-red pool.

"Off with every shred of clothes, and in we go!" he said. "Every spot on your bodies, even your hair, must be Indian."

The plan Cliff had suggested in Amadale, and which had been accepted by Mr. Whitley, and, later, by Bill, depended upon a complete disguise so that they could don the native garb, even the robes and ornaments of Inca nobles, later and not be suspected.

Into the turgid pool they plunged. Nicky, who rather hated cold water, was the only one who did not dive in, so to speak. He dipped a toe and they all roared as he drew it out. "Red-toe!" Cliff shouted. "Nicky-Nicky Red-toe!"

"Well, you needn't talk! Who ever saw an Inca with a white man's head."

They bantered and chaffed him as he gradually dipped in and then Tom caught Nicky off his guard and dragged him in, all-over! He tried to duck Tom in return, and they made a game of it until Mr. Whitley warned them against the danger of their shouts being heard.

When, after carefully inspecting one another and being certain that not even a part in their hair would show a break in the rich, deep, copper-brownish red of the vegetable dye which penetrated their pores but had no ill effects, they stood around in the sunshine, drying.

The surprise to them all was the effect which the dye had on Cliff. His light, tow-colored hair had come out a rich, glistening and beautiful reddish golden color!

"Glory to gramma!" Nicky laughed. "Wouldn't that be lovely if you were a girl? Those curls! Those ringlets! Those golden red curlies!"

"At that," said Bill soberly, turning Cliff around as he inspected. "This is going to turn out well for us."

"Turn out well? How?" inquired Mr. Whitley.

"We won't go as simple natives wandering in by mistake, as we had planned," Bill said. "Do you happen to remember anything about the Inca religion?"

"Why, yes," they all chorused, beginning to dress in the simple, but bright wool robes Bill had selected before they left Cuzco and which looked very well with their deeply toned skin.

"They worshipped the Sun," Tom said. "They built temples to the Sun."

"More than that," Bill added. "To them the Sun was the visible symbol of the god they worshipped, Raymi. But they also believed that the moon was the wife of the Sun, and that such stars as they could see were like a retinue or court of pages to wait on the royal Sun and his moon-wife."

"Yes," Cliff broke in, "I know, or I think I know, what you are about to say. They called Venus—wait, now, let me get it!——"

Nicky was bouncing up and down on a rock. Finally he could contain himself no longer.

"Chasqui!" he said excitedly.

"No," said Tom with contempt, "'Chasqui' means a runner—like the chap who carried that quipu."

Nicky looked crestfallen, but Cliff smiled.

"You were close," he admitted, "and you reminded me of what I wanted to say.

"Venus was the favorite star of the Incas and they called her 'Chaska'—that was like saying 'Page of the Sun' but I guess that is a pretty free translation." He turned to Bill.

"Not too free," Bill grinned. "But it really meant just exactly what you are at this moment—'the youth with the flowing and shining locks!'"

"Why, yes," said Mr. Whitley, "I remember that. And it will fit in splendidly. Cliff, from now on, if all goes well, you shall be 'Chaska—Page of the Sun!'"

And, as they made final plans, on their rock, the rush-roofed quarters of Huascar Inca Capac, ruler of hidden Quichaka, were invaded by two unshod men—none wore sandals in the presence of their ruler!—who bowed to the floor.

"We make report," said the taller man. "Oh, Inca—" and a stream of titles and words of praise followed.

"Let it be spoken from the tongues of truth," said the Inca.

They bowed again and the story of the exodus into the strange outer world was told. He who had been silent related his experiences on a journey to that strange continent where all men were pale and where many monsters with hot breath and coughing voices dragged great rolling houses along on hard roads of shining metal; where houses were, oh! piled one upon another until one could not count them to the top; where men had even trained huge birds whose wings did not move but whose voices were as the roar of an avalanche, so that these birds did rise from earth to carry the men through the air. Thus, and with many other strange stories he explained to the wondering ruler the sights he had seen but that he did not understand. How could he, buried in his mountain retreat, explain a railway train, or the high skyscrapers of America, or its aeroplanes?

"And the letter of the captive?" demanded the Inca.

Its story also was told up to the arrival of the party among the snows of the white pass.

"There we flung rocks upon them, and we believe that all ran back except one who lay still until new snow covered him."

The Inca commended their splendid work.

"But this I do not understand," said he who had been to America, and he displayed the quipu of Bill Sanders. "I sent a message to my brother in the hills and on the way it changed from a message of warning, that men came, to this."

"Read it, quipucamayu," the Inca commanded of the other.

"It tells, oh Inca, of the coming of one from the stars, yes, even of Chasca, Page of the Sun, himself, as our fathers prophecied so many ages ago."

"Strange," mused the ruler. "And last night a star flew from the East to the West and fell into darkness." The natives of many lands are as superstitious about the marvels of nature as were the Incas. "Is it a good omen, think you?"

"Royal Inca, son of the Sun," answered his priest, "when the royal Atahualpa was on the eve of capture by the men of white faces, it is told by our haravecs—poets, minstrels—that a star fell!"

"Even so," growled the Inca, "if Chasca comes to spell my doom, I care not whether he come from the Sun or from Cupay—the god of evil—I will sink an arrow into his flesh!"

"Not so!" the priest of the Sun was shaking with suppressed dismay. "Oh, Inca, royal though you be, say not thus."

"How be, if I am of the Sun a son—shall I then fear one of his vassals—a page?"

The other noble, a high councillor, spoke softly.

"Fear not, Inca, neither anger the messenger. When gods begin to fling arrows other gods may be stronger—or weaker."

That evening, just before the moon rose from behind the cliff on which they camped, Tom and Nicky crouched over a tiny electric battery.

"There's Bill's signal," whispered Tom. Nicky closed a switch.

"Come, Incas, come and watch your first fireworks display!" chuckled Nicky. "I hope it works!" he added.

In the far city, as the ruddy glow grew on the hilltop, men watching the stars sent word to the Inca of the strange sight. The populace was flat on its collective faces, half terrified, half awed at the red fire shining brightly far to the East; as it died down they saw the silver moon peep at them.

And late that night came runners to gasp out their news: in that terror-fire they had seen outlined a figure of black, its arms stretched wide, and on its head a glory of shining hair!

Through the city the news fled from the nobles to their subjects!

"Chasca! Page of the Sun! He has come!"

And at least one Chasca was sound asleep that that very moment.

CHAPTER XI
"CHASCA HAILLI!"

Before the peaks they had crossed were lit by the first hint of morning light, Cliff and his fellows were busy. Already, during the day past, they had selected a sturdy tree with a stout bough projecting over the cliff edge. To this bough Tom and Nicky climbed before break of day on this eventful morning and to the top of the limb, after making a beginning with a large nail, hammered in a little way, they began to screw home a very strong pulley. Gripping the bough, steadying each other, they twisted the screw home until the pulley was safely secured.

Cliff flung an end of the light, strong rope they had brought and as it hissed upward Tom caught it and thrust its end through the pulley sheaves, drew more of it through and then, with Nicky, descended to the ground.

Their problem had been to be able to return to the top of this sheer precipice when their mission would be accomplished. For that purpose careful plans had been made and were being carried out.

In a sort of harness of the rope, at one end, Bill and Mr. Whitley affixed a heavy slab of stone; this they lowered over the sheer wall and let the rope pay out until the stone thudded to a stop far below them.

"That stone makes a counter-balance," Bill stated. "Now we make a large loop at this upper end of our rope—so! Take your seat in it, John," to Mr. Whitley, "we put the pack in your lap and you grip it with your knees. Now the rock makes it easy for us to lower you. Going down!"

When the rock came slowly and easily into their reach, its weight making it simple for them to control the descent of the other end, they waited until a double tug on the rope told them that Mr. Whitley was safe and free; they paid out and the rock slipped back into the darkness.

"You next, Nicky, with your pack!"

In that way they all descended, Bill being last. He judged the weight of his own load, combined with his weight, to be about a half as much again as that of the stone; so by paying out the other side of the rope upward he let himself downward to a point where the stone came level with him; then, holding both strands tightly in one mittened hand, he hooked a prepared hook on his pack to the rope under the stone, released that side and with the stone balancing him, felt himself descending at a speed sufficiently retarded to enable them to break his landing without even a jar.

Then they fixed a stout twine to the looped end of the rope and by letting the twine pay upward, lowered stone and pack.

They next tied a fairly small rock to the low end of their twine and drew downward on the rope. In that way, they were able to recover the entire rope, having loosened its loops so that it passed through the pulley; and still they had the twine led through the upper pulley for future use. Braced against the sheer wall, Bill acted as a sort of "under-stander" for a human pillar, Cliff on his shoulders, Tom as the top man; in that high position Tom let the twine run so that the small rock's weight drew it up until the end was in his hand; he felt for, and found, a crevice into which he wedged it with a sliver of stone.

In that way they left an end of the twine too high to be discovered and removed; later they could secure it and by letting the stone at its other end pull it down, could readily affix their rope and again reave it through the pulley and get themselves back to the high point. They hid the rope carefully and began preparations for the day whose light was already dyeing the sky with vivid colors. Looking upward as the light grew stronger they saw that against the neutral rock their dull twine did not show up at all and only sharp eyes might detect the fine line high above leading over the bough. Their way of escape was quite likely to remain undisturbed.

"I only hope our plans will work out," said Mr. Whitley, as they ate a cold breakfast, not wishing to light a fire.

"If we were dealing with the Peruvians near the Pacific, or on the eastern slope, I wouldn't try it," Bill declared. "The Spaniards have educated them just a little too much to make it safe. But away off here, buried in the mountains for centuries—ever since about 1532—I feel sure that the old superstitions and beliefs still count in our favor."

They had not long to wait before discovering which way the hidden valley would deal with the intruders.

Through the field glasses Bill reported that people were moving about in distant fields and that a group seemed to be moving slowly toward them on a road which seemed to end about half a mile away, at a low stone building. To that the group proceeded.

"You had better get up on your rocks, Cliff," he suggested. "Don't pay any attention, whatever happens; just look as if you were lost in meditations."

Cliff took the position they had agreed upon and the others squatted at a little distance. Outwardly they paid no attention but Cliff saw, as did Bill, whose position enabled him to report softly to the others, that his position was the focal point for groups and solitary figures from every direction. About two hundred gathered at a respectful distance, murmuring in low tones, evidently fascinated as they watched Cliff.

"If I have figured right," Bill told Tom and Nicky, "in just about two minutes the sun will be high enough."

"High enough for what?" asked Nicky.

"I think I know," Tom told him; but Bill signed for quiet and from the corners of their eyes they kept watch of Cliff. He stood without moving, a veritable statue of an Indian in his gaily colored robe which Cliff had been assured by Bill was a garment of the sort worn by the nobles.

Several minutes passed and then the sun topped the rim of the ledge and flung its rays downward; slowly the shadow crept back until, almost as if a curtain had been drawn away, the sun shaft fell upon Cliff's head. It lighted up the reddish gold that the dye had made of his hair, and at the sight, from the clustered natives came a deep murmur.

"Chasca—Chasca—as the prophecy told!—the youth with bright and flowing locks!" And then a roar, "Chasca—Hailli! Hailli!" It was a cry of mingled triumph and respect.

"It works well," Bill said, and slowly rose.

He stepped forward slowly. The natives melted into a more compact mass and gave ground a pace; but Bill made a sign that they seemed to understand. He made a brief oration; the others listened silently. Then several detached themselves and with incredibly swift legs, sped away toward the distant city.

"Turn as though you were in a dream and stroll into the tent," Bill told Cliff. He obeyed.

"No use letting the novelty wear off," Bill grinned to Mr. Whitley. "And, besides, I want him ready to make a grand entrance, sort of the way they do in the circus."

"Grand entry? To what?" Nicky was still lost in the mazes of this unusual procedure.

"To ride to town with the Inca!" Bill chuckled.

Sure enough, about noon, by which time the crowd around their location had trebled in numbers, a procession was seen on the road.

When it reached them the young fellows stared, hiding their surprise at Bill's muttered warning. Many soldiers, with bows and arrows, some with curious looking swords, came first; they separated into two lines, to the right and to the left; through the lane advanced many tall, erect men in colorful garments.

These advanced and stopped in a little group. Behind them other men carrying two gorgeous litters, one a little more gaudy than the other, set down their shafts and rested.

What Bill said as he advanced to parley with several men who came a few steps toward him, the other members of the party could not hear. Presently he returned.

"I told them we are servants of the royal and heaven-sent Chasca, who has been sent to bless their land; they seemed to like it. That second 'hamaca' is for Cliff."

He moved close to the tent.

While he pretended to bow and to remove his shoes, and to go through some sort of rites which made Nicky want to laugh, Bill whispered to Cliff.

"Can you hear me, Cliff?"

"Yes."

"When I say 'Hailli, Chasca' the third time, open the tent flap. Pay no attention to anybody. Don't answer if anybody speaks. Keep yourself erect and act as though everybody here was dirt under your feet. Got all that?"

"Yes, Bill."

"Pick out the biggest of the two litters and walk right to it as if you knew all about it. Stop by it and just bow your head forward a little and say, 'Hailli, Inca!' and then turn and let the bearers help you into the other hamaca. Don't talk, and don't notice anything. I'll do everything—with John."

Presently the tent flaps separated and out came the counterfeit of the supposed celestial visitor. He did as Bill had instructed him. To the litter, which was covered with gold, or gold leaf, and heavily ornamented with green stones and other glittering gems, he made his solemn, unhurried way.

"Hailla, Inca!"

"Chasca, Hailli," answered a deep voice from within. Cliff saw a man reclining, in royal robes, of texture even finer than the robes worn by those around him; on his head was a circle of fringed wool, the scarlet "borla" or sign of the Inca, with its two feathers from the sacred birds which were kept to supply those feathers alone-two of them to be worn by the Inca in his headgear. Huge golden ornaments hung so heavily from the man's ears that they had dragged his earlobes down practically to his shoulders. He was a strange looking person and yet there was dignity and solemn power in his face.

While Cliff was helped to ascend to the floor of his own litter, Nicky had a little experience of his own.

Several llamas, the native sheep, that is the largest of the four varieties, whose wool was the most coarse and used only for the garments of the subjects—

the nobles got the finer wools!—had been brought up. They were the only beasts the Incas knew for burdens.

But Nicky thought they were there to be ridden!

Now a llama is a curious animal; he will carry a light burden without complaint; but if the load is heavier than he likes he will lie down and he won't get up until the load is lightened.

Nicky flung the strap which was fastened between two small packs over the llama's back and then, with a hop, was up there himself.

Thereupon the beast lay down promptly. Nicky shouted and slapped its woolly side, but it made a queer little grunt and lay still. The natives broke into shouts of laughter, as also did Tom and Bill as the latter hastened to explain to Nicky that he must walk.

Cliff had seen the little incident and he had hard work to avoid laughing; but he maintained sober gravity and soon the caravan was ready and moved slowly toward the road; first the soldiers, then the nobles, or priests perhaps; then came Bill and John Whitley walking at either side of Cliff's litter; after them were Nicky and Tom, and then a regular throng of natives chanting and singing.

"Don't ask about the white man—your father—too soon," Bill warned Cliff softly. "It might arouse suspicion. But we're on our way to Quichaka and I hope we find your pa well and wise."

"So do I," muttered Cliff, "I can hardly wait!"

It was a slow but interesting journey to Quichaka. The youths feasted their eyes on strange scenes. The valley was laid out in splendid farms, with many vegetables that were not easy to recognize, although great fields of maize or corn could easily be identified. The road was beautifully smooth, of great flat stones laid straight and level. Once they passed over a bridge of huge stonework piles, with heavy timbers laid across to support the flat slabs of the roadway.

Finally they came into the city. It was spread out widely, and, as Bill estimated later, probably had a population of some eight or ten thousand. In the poorer quarters the houses were of a rude clay-like composition, much like the *adobe* of Mexico; the finer homes were of stones, large and small, rough for the most part, but with their edges, where they joined, smooth and so closely matched that the joints were hard to detect; they had no windows; the Incas did not know about glass. The doors were open in the temperate noonday and early afternoon warmth; within there was too much gloom to show the furnishings.

Straight streets, laid out in perfect parallels and with exactly right angled cross streets, finally took them to a great square in the center of the city; there were massive, but only single-story buildings all about. At one side were what appeared to be the quarters of the ruler and of his chief nobles. On the other were public buildings whose nature was not readily seen.

At the far end of the square was a massive building which could be discerned as the temple. It was almost a duplicate of the description that histories gave of the Sun Temple in Cuzco, once capital of the Inca empire; the one in Quichaka had the same ornamented exterior with a cornice of shining gold plates.

Groups had lined the farmland along the road; in the suburbs the crowds had been greater.

In the square there seemed to be almost the whole population of the city, massed at either side. They took up the chant as the party progressed and the sound grew to a roar.

At the open space before the temple to the Sun they all stopped and the Inca descended.

Mounting the steps of a smaller building, which Bill whispered was, as its silver ornaments showed, the temple to the Moon, he made a declamation which the youths' understanding of the dialect called quichua enabled them to understand partly; he welcomed Chasca, messenger of the Sun, come to earth to give plenty and happiness to their land.

"See that small temple at one side," Bill muttered to Cliff. There were about five of the smaller buildings around the greater temple; one for priests, one dedicated to the stars, another to Illapa—general term for thunder, lightning, all the forces of nature which they also reverenced—as well as the larger one dedicated to the Moon. Bill nodded toward that which was sacred to Venus and other stars. Cliff agreed. "If they ask us or give us a chance to choose, pick that one," Bill muttered. "It fits the part you are playing—it is the star temple."

The populace greeted the Inca's talk with shouts and cries of delight. Then a priest, in finely wrought robes, advanced and spoke to Bill; they all seemed to maintain a reverent air and hesitated to address Cliff directly. Bill nodded and told his comrades they were to be housed in the temple of the stars.

There they were led and young girls of a pretty red-bronze, with long black hair, came to attend to their wants while the crowds outside shouted and applauded until the door was shut.

"You have come at a good time," said the priest who had come in with Bill, "He-Who-Comes-From-the-Stars can destroy the crawling things that eat up our corn."

"Is it, then, blighted?" Bill asked. The priest stared at him and Bill read his mind: celestial messengers should know everything. Bill smiled grimly and corrected his blunder.

"You must know, O, noble of the High-and-Sacred-Order, we who come to earth to serve Chasca must lose the wisdom of the stars and the youth with the bright and shining locks has not chosen to tell us of his purpose among you."

He glanced toward Cliff who was keeping apart from them and added: "Now we would have food and then we would be alone and I will speak of this matter of the corn to Chasca."

"It shall be so," replied the priest and issued orders to the girls who began to busy themselves bringing rude tables and utensils into the small antechamber of the temple where they were to be quartered.

"And if there are those who are sick," went on Bill, "name them to me that Chasca may be asked to smile toward them and, if it is his purpose, lift them from the ground."

"There is one—but he is only a pale and worthless one, not of our tribe, though quite a scholar. But first, O, servant speak of our corn."

"It shall be so," said Bill. "Now—leave us."

While they ate strange meats and other food from dishes of silver and gold, served by the maidens, Bill told Cliff that he knew that the father they had come to help was alive. They were all glad and anxious to find a way to see him.

"I wonder why those girls keep tittering, and looking at Nicky," said Tom as the dishes were cleared away.

Bill, smiling to himself, beckoned to one and said a few words in quichua. The girl giggled, quite like any girl, put her finger to her lips shyly and then whispered a swift word and fled.

Bill broke into a hearty laugh.

"All right for you!" grumbled Nicky. "They have some joke about me. If you don't want to tell——"

"They have a name for you," Bill chuckled. "Never mind the exact word, but it means He-Who-Sits-Down-Upon-Llamas!"

CHAPTER XII
CLIFF FACES A PROBLEM

"You fellows are having all the fun," Cliff said ruefully, while the disguised five sat around after dinner the third day they spent in Quichaka. "You can go all over town and see all the sights and I have to sit like a judge, all alone in my temple."

"It won't be for long," Nicky cheered him up. "Bill saw your father again—how was he, Bill?"

"He's getting better every minute," Bill informed them. "When they took me to see him first—at Chasca's command—and I don't think they suspected anything—I managed to get a chance to whisper to him that we were disguised friends. He chirked up right away. He isn't so very sick—just weak. He lost hope and heart, I guess, and sort of pined away. But today I got a chance to whisper that his son is here—you ought to see him spruce up!"

"If I could see him——" Cliff said.

"It would be dangerous. Either he, or you, might get excited and spoil everything. No! Better wait till the Feast of Raymi. Then we can have him brought before you. He's pretending that he is no better so that when you see him you can pretend to cure him."

"I think that will be best," counselled Mr. Whitley. "Now if you are ready, Tom, let us go out to the farm lands and inspect that corn crop again. I am something of a chemist and I think that if I can only find the ingredients to mix a good insecticide, we can show them what will seem like a marvelous destruction of the pests which are eating away the grain. We must search as quickly as we can because we want to be ready at the festival."

They went away toward the outlying farms and grain fields. Mr. Whitley wanted to see exactly what insects were at work, then he felt sure that he could discover some means of ending their depredations.

Cliff sat in moody silence for a time.

"That girl who always laughs at me and calls me the fellow who sits down on llamas," Nicky broke the silence. "She is a nice girl, even if she does laugh. She told me there is going to be a big competition—I don't quite understand what kind—races or something. Why can't Cliff enter the race and then he could train and get out for exercise."

Bill offered to find out what was to occur, and went away. He came back very soon and informed Cliff that before the annual Feast of Raymi, the great festival in honor of their sun-god, the Inca would choose from among his sons the one who should be the next Inca.

Such young nobles were carefully trained during a long period of preparation; they were taught the arts of war as the Incas understood them; they were also taught many other things, and then, at an appropriate time, great games and competitions were held in which endurance, prowess and skill were tested.

Such a contest was to be held very soon, just before the great festival. Challcuchima, one of the ruler's many sons—for the Inca had many wives and many children—was ready to receive the ceremonials of appointment. Cliff, as Chasca, had already received and commended Challcuchima; a fine, clean-limbed fellow near Cliff's age, the young Indian made a good impression.

"I had a chat with Inca Capac," Bill said. "I hinted that it was in the mind of Chasca to become as a mortal youth and try his skill against the noble youths and the son who is the Inca's favorite. He liked the idea."

"Then we will change the temple of the stars into training quarters," Nicky said excitedly, springing up. "I'd like to do some contesting too. And so would Tom, if Mr. Whitley can spare him."

When they returned, Tom and Mr. Whitley took the plan well; the young history instructor saw a splendid chance to give his young charges a real insight into Inca sports while he, with Bill, could be away in the mountains, searching for certain chemicals or ore deposits from which to extract certain mineral salts for his insecticide.

The populace learned of the coming contests and became as excited as children. They loved sports and contests; never a cruel race by nature the nobles, although they endured hardships and inflicted pain mercilessly to themselves and to enemies in war, were by nature gentle and their sports were far less cruel than those history attributes to the Spartan race, yet somewhat akin to these in some aspects.

In tests of endurance the Spartan methods were approached; already the young son of the Inca and other noble youths had been going through these. Clad in mean attire and sleeping on the ground, they had endured many hardships; among the tests was a three day fast. But that was over and there was a brief respite during which food and exercise built up strength for the climax—races, archery as they understood it with their war bows and arrows, and contests of an athletic sort.

Cliff, as Chasca, but less the supposed god than the real youth, was very popular with all the people as he walked in the temple grounds. He and Tom and Nicky strolled about, the day before the great contest, admiring the marvels all about them.

"Did you ever see so much gold and silver?" Tom exclaimed, "not only their utensils and ornament—but look there! Beyond those real flowers and that little clump of corn—there are gold and silver flowers—and all the varieties of things that they grow!"

They strolled over to examine them. Bill joined them. Mr. Whitley was busy with some minerals.

The garden they entered was an astonishing place. The Incas used precious metals as we use bronze and marble, for statues and ornaments and even duplicates in gold and silver of their garden fruits and flowers. Gold was so common in the mountains that it was not used for money; in fact the Incas had no money of any sort; they did not require it under their system of government whereby everyone was cared for by the governing tribe, so that wool, grain and other articles of daily necessity were distributed fairly and plentifully and everyone shared in the labor of their production. Therefore the precious metals were employed for other uses than that of currency.

They examined an especially beautiful parcel of corn stalks and ears of grain, executed in gold and silver; the stalks were of silver, the fat, bulging grain ears were sheathed in golden reproductions of the husk, the corn kernels peeped out, perfect and golden, while the tassel of cornsilk was made of spun silver threads. They exclaimed as they studied the wonderful workmanship and then went on to the fresh wonders—fruit and flowers so perfect that they would deceive except for their sheen of white or deep, glowing yellow.

When they turned the corner of the star-temple they stopped in surprise. In a huddled heap, a girl lay on the ground, her body shaking with sobs that racked her.

"Why," Nicky cried, "it's Caya. It's the girl who called me the fellow who sits on llamas. What's the matter, Caya?"

She sat up, her dusky face streaming with tears, and shook her head, for Nicky had forgotten and spoken in English.

Bill stepped close, squatted beside her and repeated the question. At first she only shook her head, turned away and buried her face in her arms, rocking in grief.

Finally she gasped out, in a sobbing voice, her story.

The Incas were not usually a cruel people, and it was almost unheard of for them to make a human sacrifice to their gods. But, in some great crisis of their community, they were known to resort to such methods to appease their gods.

Such a crisis was the attack of the insects upon their corn.

And they were planning a sacrifice to induce Raymi, their god, to look down with favor on their crop and destroy the menace to their future food supply.

In great buildings far from the everyday life of the tribe they kept certain chosen maidens who were employed in the service of the Sun-god, spinning and weaving tapestries, garments and ornamental cloth. From among these a sacrifice was chosen, when the rare occasion came for such a terrible need.

"They have—chosen—my—sister!" sobbed Caya.

"Goodness!" exclaimed Nicky. "We must do something to stop them."

"We can't interfere in their religious rites," warned Bill, sadly but seriously.

The girl grovelled before Cliff, as though, being the messenger from the stars he must be able to help her.

Cliff felt very badly. It was outrageous and inhuman, this thing those people planned to do.

But what could he do to stop it?

He bent down and put a hand awkwardly on the girl's black, touseled hair.

"There must be some way——" he said, looking across her head toward Bill.

"I can't see any way," Bill said morosely.

"When is this to take place?" he asked the girl in quichua.

"At the Feast of Raymi!" she sobbed.

"Well, you stop crying and——" Bill nudged him. Cliff, too, was using English. He hesitated, and Bill lifted the slim, quivering girl to her feet.

"Be not afraid, child of the long and curling locks," he said kindly in the dialect she understood, "Chasca does not wish to see your eyes wet. But what can be done, Chasca will do; but breathe not a word lest Chasca's pity turn to wrath!"

She dropped to the ground and struck her forehead on the path, to Cliff's great dismay. Then as she remained in that abased position he touched his chums' arms and they, with Bill, silently slipped away.

"Run and tell Mr. Whitley," he urged Tom. "If he can get his chemicals ready in time we may save Caya's sister."

"But if he can't?" said Nicky desperately.

Cliff shrugged helplessly.

"I don't know," he said.

CHAPTER XIII
THE GAMES

"Come on, you Tom! Oh, Tom—come on!" Nicky shouted and screeched above the roar of excitement. Neck and neck, down a circling path beaten in the stubby grass, Tom and an Indian raced, stride for stride; behind them came a fleet following.

"Come on, Tom," said Cliff, under his breath; he had to fight down his desire to shout; he was Chasca and must remember his pose.

Near the finish came the racers. Shouts and cries of encouragement drowned Nicky's shrill yells.

But Tom put forth his remaining burst of strength and with scarcely three inches to his credit, flitted over the mark—winner in the race in which all the young nobles contested except the Inca's son alone.

Not far beyond Quichaka there was a sudden rise of the hills in front of whose sharp slope a large tract had been leveled off. From early dawn the lesser natives had streamed to their places on the hillside, and after an early and ample breakfast Cliff and his companions had gone forth with the Inca and his retinue, Cliff being honored by a seat in a hamaca, as had been his fortune on their arrival. He and Bill, Mr. Whitley and Nicky, sat near one another, watching Tom in the foot races. Cliff sat in the place of honor at one side of the Inca whose other place on the further side was given to the high priest of the temple of the Sun. Below them, among the nobles, were his friends.

By his victory over the nobles Tom eliminated all competition and would, after a rest, have to race Challcuchima—and it had been privately agreed among the youths of Cliff's party that they might all best the nobles but it would be an act of wisdom to allow the Inca's favorite son to be the final victor in any contest except those in which Cliff, himself a "son of the stars" would compete—there, since the Inca was claimed to be of celestial descent, the contest might fall to whom the Fates and skill should decree. So, later, Tom failed to exert his utmost speed, although he felt that by doing so he might have tied, if not outdistanced, Challcuchima.

To the surprise of all the assembled natives, but not so much to that of his friends, Nicky came off victor—except against Challcuchima—in tests with bow and arrow. While the willow of his own archery outfit was lighter than the stout war bows, even in the size which the youths of sixteen employed, his arm was sturdy and his eye was well trained.

Then came battles with swords, very much like those used in actual fighting; of course their edges were blunted and their points rounded off; nevertheless in the earnest thrust and swing of the mimic contests, several accidents of guard resulted in thrusts that came near to being fatal; in these contests the three chums were spectators.

Then came matched wrestlers and there Cliff was in his element; wrestling, under fair rules, he loved; in its clever and strength-testing grips and stresses he was a master.

Although they approached their supposedly celestial antagonist in some awe and perhaps because of that feeling did not use their best skill, nevertheless Cliff had several very arduous and breath-taxing struggles with young nobles; but each he finally laid neatly down with both shoulders touching the sward.

inally he vanquished his third antagonist and threw himself down, panting. There were cheers and, with eyes turned, he saw that Challcuchima had just completed his own final test with a noble's son. These two, if they came off victors in their respective combats, were to rest and then strive for the final victory.

The time came and the two, evenly matched in weight and with equally quick eyes and well matched skill, took their position on the grass. Cliff, of the two, had the disadvantage that he had not been in athletic training as long as had Challcuchima and was, therefore, the more tired at the end of his three bouts.

However, he had no fear or dismay in his mind. At the word of their Indian referee, the youths came together, seeking for best holds and advantages.

Cliff got a surprise. Hands gripping each others arms, straining for a chance to slip quick muscles into knots when the right hold could be won, Cliff felt his antagonist go suddenly as limp as a rag. Challcuchima seemed to be sagging, as if he were weak and was about to fall. Cliff was startled enough to let go in order to catch the youth and prevent a fall. To his dismay Challcuchima was on the very instant a steel spring and a panther for quickness and before his adversary could recover the ruler's son had caught him with arms that steadily bent the American youth backward for the throw; but Cliff, in his turn, played a surprise trick, for he let his legs go straight out from under him so that instead of being forced down he was falling backward. That threw his weight on Challcuchima's wrist and the hold broke; Cliff twisted in air as he felt the lock break, so that while Challcuchima fought to regain his stand his opponent landed on all fours and was up and sliding his hands up as Challcuchima caught his arms.

The pace slowed then; each realized that he could gain little by tricks that were more acrobatic than wrestling. The half sneering curl left Challcuchima's lips, however, and a look of considerable respect was in his eyes as they strove and strained, hands slipping, gripping muscles tensing and flexing, sinews straining to the turn and twist of their supple bodies.

As in the first strife the trickery of one was met by the quick thought and agility of the other, so, during the long minutes, for they wrestled continuously from start to final defeat of one or the other, each saw himself equaled. When Challcuchima secured the Inca equivalent of a half-nelson, Cliff knew how to create overconfidence and eventually disarm the holder and himself get an advantage; when he seized a fortunate instant to drive through into a hammerlock, Challcuchima had a trick that made Cliff's teeth snap in the pain of suddenly stressed muscles and he had to release. For it seemed that each of them knew some principles of the science of causing a surprise reflex by some hold that taxed a sensitive nerve more than a straining muscle; and both used their knowledge.

Finally, wearied by strain and exertion they stood, arm to arm, panting, eyeing one another and then the Inca rose and spoke.

"Thus must end the contest," he told them, "the son of an Inca, himself descended from the god we worship, can not hope to put down Chasca, himself holy and from the stars. Nor can Chasca put down the son of the master he has come to visit in friendship."

"Even so, royal Father," panted Challcuchima. "We were evenly matched."

Cliff smiled queerly, turning his head away; his chums wondered why. The rest of the ceremonial was rather tedious; long and flowery speeches were made by the Inca and his chief priest, extolling the virtues of his son and exhorting him to carry the wise and generous rule forward when he became Inca. Garlands were placed on the heads of all the contestants, made of bright flowers with evergreen woven into that of Challcuchima to show his endurance. Then he was crowned with the special, tasseled fillet of vicuna wool, yellow in color, which attested his appointment to be the next ruler.

When the ceremonies were over and, back in their temple, the contenders and Bill and Mr. Whitley discussed the previous events Tom turned to Cliff.

"Why did you smile at the Inca's decision—when you and Chally wrestled to a standstill?" he demanded.

"He bribed me," Cliff answered. "Remember, when I had the hammerlock hold——?"

"I wondered how he broke that," Nicky interrupted and Bill nodded.

"He whispered that if I defeated him he would be disgraced, and promised to give me anything I wanted if I would not win."

"Did you make him promise anything?" Nicky was eager.

"No—but I will."

"Oh!" Nicky was quick to see the idea in Cliff's mind. "At the Feast of Raymi—before the sacrifice—Caya's sister."

"Yes, if Mr. Whitley doesn't get his chemicals to save the corn." Nicky turned a handspring, with a hurrah!

CHAPTER XIV
GOLD, AND A SURPRISE

"Four days more and you will see your father," Bill told Cliff. "He is much better. I saw him today."

"If only I could slip away and see him, just for a minute." Cliff spoke wistfully. Bill shook his head.

"I am afraid they would suspect something," he said. "It was easy for me to see him, as I told you before; I pretended to know that there was a great, pale scholar from beyond the mountains whose knowledge I wanted to compare with mine. The chief priest often talked with your pa and he was glad to take me; and now I can go alone. You are supposed to be spending all your time pleading with the Sun-god to save their corn. I'm afraid to have you caught going through the tunnels."

Quichaka was a city modeled very closely along the pattern of the ancient capital, Cuzco. As in that old place, so in Quichaka, the grounds beneath the temples were honeycombed with secret passages, tunnels that led to underground chambers.

In the fifteenth century Topa Inca Yapanqui had extended the borders of the flourishing empire of the Incas to the Maule River and his son had later subdued Quito and made it a part of his possessions; then the Spaniards had come into the country. Observing that these invaders had confiscated treasure, one of the many sons of the reigning Inca of the period had gathered much treasure and many of his nobles and their subjects and had found a way to the hidden valley where they had built up Quichaka during long years of labor until it almost duplicated the ancient glories of Cuzco, their former home.

"They don't keep Cliff's father in a dungeon, do they?" Tom asked Bill. Mr. Whitley was away, alone, in the foothills, searching for certain minerals. Bill shook his head in reply to Tom.

"Not a dungeon," he explained. "They have some cells down under the ground but he is in a sort of chamber, a good, big room."

"Why isn't he allowed to be in a house?" Nicky demanded.

Huamachaco, the high priest, is to blame for that," Bill said. "Cliff's pa heard in some way that there was a secret pass or some way to get out of the valley and he tried to find it; they caught him and brought him back and then he tamed the eaglet and when they discovered that it was missing and found some torn scraps of paper which he had tried to destroy after he had spoiled the letter he had started on them, Huamachaco, who isn't any man's dummy, decided to have the white man watched."

It was because the chief priest was so clever that Bill feared to take the least chance of upsetting their plans.

Challcuchima, who had become very much attached to Cliff and to his chums, in a respectful awed way, came to visit them while they discussed their plans.

"Holy Chasca," he said to Cliff in quichua dialect at which Cliff was only fairly proficient, covering up his deficiency by saying very little. "As successor to the Inca rule I have been shown the mysteries of the secret ways beneath the city. Among our hidden treasure is a statue which is like you and yet not like you. My father, the Inca, has permitted me to show it to you that you may say if it is truly your image and if it should be set in the Temple of the Stars."

Cliff consulted Bill with his eyes and Bill, with a very tiny wink and nod, bade him go. The chums, not invited, looked downcast as Cliff walked across the gardens of gold and silver with his young guide; but Bill soothed them by telling them what he had seen underground.

Cliff was to see far more than was permitted to the eyes of his supposed scholarly servant.

Taking him to the Inca, who greeted him with a mixed respect and good feeling, Challcuchima led Cliff through a tapestried and hidden opening in the private rooms of the palace; then they went down many steps; Cliff had brought a flashlight, an implement which caused Challcuchima much awe and wonder when he was allowed to operate it. Mostly, they used torches as they traversed long passages, twisted around sharp bends, slipped through cross-cuts.

Finally the two came to a huge chamber cut out of the rock. Servants, carrying torches, held their lights high and Cliff had to suppress his tendency to gasp. He had never seen a sight to compare with that which met his eyes.

"This is the room beneath the Temple of the Sun," Challcuchima informed him, "this is sacred ground." He and Cliff removed their sandals for everyone of the few permitted access to the Temple or its underground counterpart, went unshod.

Wide and long was the chamber. The light, flaring and flickering as the torches leaped up and burned down, was filled with gold and silver objects. There were utensils of every sort, from plates, cups and rude pots, to wonderful statues and urns and placques of precious metal. It was a very treasure-house.

Challcuchima led Cliff, his eyes dazed by the glories of the objects which he dared only to examine briefly in passing, to a statue depicting a youth cast and moulded in purest gold, a lithe, poised figure of a young man in the action of running, poised on the toes of one foot, the other leg thrust out and lifted as though it had just taken a step.

"It is like to you and yet not like," said Challcuchima.

Cliff thought quickly. It could not be a trap, this effort to discover whether or not he knew the figure. Or could it. And why a trap at all? Was anyone suspicious of his pose and of the part he played?

If he said it was Chasca and the Incas knew differently, he mused, he would disclose his ignorance: if he denied that it was the image of Venus as they imaged the god of that star, what might they answer?

He was spared the need for an answer.

Huamachaco, the high priest, coming down the passage with a torch, said something in quite an excited manner. Challcuchima grasped Cliff's arm.

"There is something new—come," he urged, "this can wait!"

Cliff hurried after the servants with their torches and his royal young guide turned swiftly into a passage they had not used, which brought them out into one of the small houses just beyond the Sun temple, a dwelling of one of the priests.

There was a crowd assembled near the Temple of the Stars and Cliff saw at once that Bill, Nicky and Tom were on the way to join the gathering crowd. With Challcuchima and Huamachaco he went quickly toward them.

"What goes on?" he asked. Huamachaco did not answer. He was rather stout and the climb had taxed his wind.

Cliff met his comrades at the edge of the group: some fell back respectfully to give passage to the young Inca-to-be and to Chasca and the high priest. They pressed to the point of interest.

A native, much more stocky than the others they had seen, and of a far deeper reddish complexion, seemed to be a captive; but so rapid was the exchange of conversation, so sharp the questions which Huamachaco asked and so hasty the replies that Cliff and his fellows were completely at sea.

Finally the crowd grew so thick that, at the high priest's order soldiers formed a quick wedge and began to disperse them. The stranger stared fixedly for a while at the group facing him, while he replied to Huamachaco's sharp demands with fluent quichua dialect. The priest seemed puzzled. Finally he made a sign to Challcuchima who turned and hurried toward his father's palace. Huamachaco, taking the stranger by the arm, with the soldiers closing in behind them, apologized to Chasca for leaving so abruptly, and Huamachaco led the stranger away toward another building.

"He claims that he has an important word for Manco Huayna, who was, he says, the fellow who went out into the mountains to find out about the eaglet," Bill explained as they returned soberly to their own place. "Do you know who I think he is?"

"The Spaniard," said Nicky promptly, "Did you see his shifty eyes?"

"Did he recognize us?" Tom asked, "I know he stared."

"I think he suspected," Bill answered.

"What word do you think he has? About us?" Tom mused.

"I hope not," said Bill, dubiously. "He's after gold, of course. I don't know how far that fellow would go in an effort to get it."

And not even Chasca could tell him.

CHAPTER XV
THE FEAST OF RAYMI

"Well, anyhow, our three day fast is over," Cliff yawned as Bill shook him awake, long before dawn. He was sleepy; but he was more hungry than he was drowsy. They had decided to carry out all of the rites of this, the greatest festival of the Inca religion; it began with three fast days which were now past.

"I wonder what has happened to Mr. Whitley," Tom said as he drew on his robe.

"I hope he comes back before the ceremony gets to the place where we have to try to stop the sacrifice," Nicky whispered. "I don't know whether the Inca's son can stop it or not, even if Cliff reminds him of his promise."

"Nor I," said Bill. "His pa would probably back him up to give comrade Cliff any gold or maybe," and his eyes would have been seen to be twinkling in a better light than that of their torch, "or, maybe, a dozen wives for the youth with the shining locks."

"Wives!" Cliff said it disgustedly. "What would I ask for wives for?"

"You might ask for Caya, anyway," Nicky said mischievously. The girl who had been assigned to serve Nicky had transferred all her attention to Cliff since Nicky had whispered, against Bill's advice, the hint that Chasca would save her sister from the sacrifice.

"She does act like a girl getting ready to 'love, honor and disobey' her lord and master," chuckled Bill.

Cliff shrugged his shoulders. She was a nice Indian girl, but his mind was not set on girls. He looked forward to the moment when he could see his father. "I'll ask for her for you, Nicky," he challenged, "you seem to be broken hearted about her."

Nicky stopped just in time—he had been about to fling a golden cup at Cliff: Challcuchima came in after knocking at the doorway of the anteroom in which they slept.

"All is ready," he greeted, seriously, "come."

They followed him into the great square. The dawn had not yet come: just a faint streak of light gray cut the darkness in the East.

"The greatest crowd I ever saw here!" exclaimed Nicky, "Look how they pack the square!" He was right. With torches that lit the place with weird gleams and deep shadows, probably every human being who could walk was there. Challcuchima led the party to a spot just beyond the crowd, in front of the

Inca's home: there they were greeted seriously and in a low tone by the high priest and the Inca.

"I don't see the stranger—the fellow we think is Sancho Pizzara," Cliff whispered. Bill shook his head.

"I wonder what he came to tell them—and where he is?" Nicky said under his breath. Since no one knew he got no reply.

The torches were gradually extinguished as the stragglers filled every available bit of room. Gradually the light was growing in the East; from pale gray it went through the slow changes of dull green, then brighter green, altering to greenish yellow and brighter lemon; then dashes of crimson came, like lances of fire flung across the sky.

A low murmur began; constantly it increased in volume and in eagerness; for it was a chant of triumph and greeting to the orb of day which they worshipped as the visible sign that their god smiled upon them. Watching, Cliff saw the first rim of the sun peep up over the peaks. There rose a vast, throaty roar of triumph and the mass of people bowed themselves toward the symbol of their deity.

"What would they do if it turned out cloudy?" Nicky wondered.

"They would take it as a bad sign for the coming year," Bill told him. He looked around anxiously. "I wish I knew where John Whitley keeps himself."

"So do I!" Tom whispered.

Challcuchima touched Cliff's arm. They were silent.

Along the great square moved the Inca, slowly, majestically. He was clad in a gorgeous robe of the beautiful woven fleece of the vicuna, with gorgeously dyed patterns of vivid colors running through it; on his head was the borla, that crimson fringe carrying two feathers from the sacred bird, the caraquenque—sacred to the purpose of supplying feathers for the Inca's head-dress. He wore many rich ornaments, laden with jewels, mostly emeralds, set in lavishly cut and worked golden shapes; from each earlobe hung the massive ornaments which, in years of wear, had drawn his earlobes down almost to his shoulders. Challcuchima was dressed as beautifully but he wore his yellow fringed and tasseled head-dress and his ears still were pierced by the golden bodkins which had been put there during his own festival, to remain until the flesh healed and left holes for the ornaments he might wear later on.

"We are bound for the Temple of the Sun," Bill told them. It proved to be true: outside the great temple, its golden cornice glowing brightly in the newly risen sun's rays, the procession halted. The people became silent. The priests and nobles drew aside and so did all but the Inca and Huamachaco, the high priest. Removing their sandals these two proceeded into the Temple of the Sun. No others were permitted in that sacred edifice except for purposes of cleaning and certain rites.

"I wish you'd look!" whispered Tom. From their stand they could see through the wide, open doorway. Within, the level rays of the sun made it very bright. Such marvels of gold, of ornamentation, such glorious tapestries and vivid colors had never before greeted the eyes of the four who stared, awed.

At the extreme end, where it faced the rising sun, was set a huge golden placque, a plate of gold many feet square. Its center was so carved and ornamented that it presented a rude semblance of a human face, eyes, nose, mouth: from the sides of its circle spread in every direction golden rays. It was a marvel of workmanship and of treasure.

After the Inca and his companion had performed certain rites they came out and more chants marked the resumption of the processional. They moved only a short way off, stopping again. Where they paused was an altar, a sinister object to Cliff and his comrades: they shuddered.

The chief priest advanced with some chant on his lips and began to use a strange curved mirror with which he concentrated the rays of the hot sun upon some prepared material on the altar.

"They have no fires burning during the fast days," Bill told his friends, "now the priest kindles the sacred fire with his mirror and some of it is given to certain Virgins of the Sun to guard. It is mighty serious for them if they ever dare to let the fire go out during the coming year."

The priest succeeded in securing smoking embers and then a blaze. He turned and made a sign and as he did so Cliff grew tense.

From a little distance a figure was led, heavily covered with white garments and a long, tissue-like veil.

Cliff caught Challcuchima's arm and gripped it tightly.

"What—what?" he stammered, and could not finish. He knew.

Challcuchima spoke quietly. They seldom made human sacrifices, to Raymi, but their corn was being destroyed; they hoped by this unusual proof of their religious ardor to placate the angry god.

"Remember," Cliff's voice shook and he could hardly recall the dialect he must use, "when we wrestled—you made a promise!"

Challcuchima seemed to guess what was coming. He drew back.

"I claim that promise, now—fulfil your promise," gasped Cliff.

The high priest heard the raised voice. He paused in the work he did with the fire, and walked quickly to Challcuchima. The Inca, also, turned and frowned at Cliff.

Cliff, his dialect forgotten, spoke in English.

"You shan't!" he cried, his head high, arms thrown upward as if he were veritably the young god he represented to them. "It is criminal! Chally, you promised me anything I'd ask. I ask for that innocent girl's life. Spare it— or——" He made a menacing gesture.

The high priest glowered and the Inca scowled. Challcuchima drew further away from Cliff.

"What does he say?" he asked of the priest.

Cliff, in vivid sunlight, stared at Bill. To his amazement, Bill was scratching his left ear with his middle finger!

CHAPTER XVI
THE MYSTERY BOYS HOLD COUNCIL

Never in the brief history of their order had the Mystery Boys held a session under more amazing and dangerous conditions!

For Cliff soon saw that Bill's sign was in no way mischance. With set face and earnest eyes the lanky, cunning Quipu Bill was calling for a session of the order, wherein signs would pass unknown to the hosts around them. The people were pressing closer.

Nicky nudged Cliff: Tom already had his arms folded across his chest, sign that he had entered the signal session: Nicky folded his arms. Cliff, mastering his excitement, did likewise.

What was the matter with Bill? Did he not realize how very serious the moment was? Why must he choose such a time to use the signals in whose mysteries Cliff and his friends had initiated him? Or—was it because of the danger?

ill placed his right hand negligently in his pocket—his coat pocket! That meant, "Do not speak!"

Cliff nodded slightly.

The priest and the Inca, Challcuchima and a number of nobles who had hastened closer, scowled and waited for an answer as Huamachaco sputtered, "What does this mean? What said Chasca?"

The air was electric with tension: Cliff felt it, his chums felt it; the mass of people, although they had not heard, had seen his dramatic attitude—and they felt the suspense. It was so still that they all distinctly heard the crackle of a kindled stick on the altar!

"Chasca speaks the language of the skies," Bill said, in the dialect of the nobles and priests, which was different from the quichua and which he had not taught the boys, although he understood much of it himself. "Chasca in his anger forgets that you do not speak the speech of the gods, being but mortals!"

All the while his hands were changing position unobtrusively, or his position or attitude shifted.

He dropped his right hand to his side, as he spoke, but the three chums saw that all fingers were clenched except the index finger which pointed outward and downward, hanging loosely.

That meant "Some one is coming!"

They stood with folded arms for he had asked no question and they did not wish to call attention to themselves by too many gestures. Bill was the leader: he had called for a council; whoever did so must do all the gesturing unless he asked for an answer. So they watched without appearing to do so.

"Chasca is very angry," Bill spoke on, calmly. He did it very well, Cliff had to admit to himself, almost as well as Cliff had done on that memorable occasion when they had considered admitting Mr. Whitley. He hoped Nicky would not speak as he had done then. Nicky did not mean to do that, but if he spoke now in his excitement he might upset all Bill's plans.

Bill had his hand spread out in what the Inca took for a gesture of anger against him and his priest. Really Cliff saw in it their sign that the next word would tell who was coming; it would be spelled on the fingers of Bill's other hand, hanging loosely at his side, using the simplest deaf-and-dumb alphabet.

They watched.

"W-h-i-t-l-e-y," he spelled. John Whitley!

They breathed sighs of relief.

"Chasca does not wish that a sacrifice be made," Bill spoke, "Chasca has made peace with Raymi for you. He is angered that you do not show more trust in him, a messenger of Raymi, come to give you blessings."

His two hands dropped into his trousers pockets. That meant that they must not look for whoever came. They must pay no attention. Cliff nodded.

Then Bill drew his hands free and folded his arms. At once they knew that the council of communion was over.

"Chasca has bidden his servant—he of the dark locks—to go forth and find a certain thing." Bill went on in the nobles' dialect, "behold—that servant returns!"

The boys did not look up, mindful of their orders; but all the others in the group did so. Through the crowd came pushing John Whitley. They made way for him but so dense was the press that he moved only slowly. Bill must have seen him signal from the outskirts of the crowd, Cliff guessed; it was true.

But what would Mr. Whitley say? Had he found what he wanted? Or—not! And would he understand the danger into which Cliff had been forced when Challcuchima failed to keep his word?

Then they saw that Bill's ear was causing him a seemingly great lot of trouble; his middle finger scratched industriously as John Whitley approached. Would he recall the signal?

"This is sacrilege!" cried the high priest. "Chasca, son of the skies, will not seek to change the rites to which we and our fathers have bowed ever since Manco Capac, founder of our line, sunk his golden wedge near Titicaca and began his rule!"

"Chasca does seek to change no rites," Bill replied calmly. "Chasca seeks to save a life because there is no need for its sacrifice!" He kept working at his ear. John Whitley broke into the circle.

"What?—" he began. He stared around. There was a moment of intense silence. A stick fell and crackled on the altar: among the maidens of the Sun there was stifled sobbing from Caya, close beside her sister but not daring to touch her!

John Whitley's eyes seemed caught by Bill's finger: he stared. Then he looked at Cliff and suddenly he folded his arms!

"Let the sacrifice proceed!" shouted the high priest, jealous of his position.

"Not so!" shouted Bill.

His fist came down into an open palm as though to emphasize his cry, but John Whitley divined that in the secret sign manual a question was being asked! "Did you get it?"

"Yes!" his right finger rubbed his chin.

"Ah," said Bill, and his voice rang out clearly as he faced the high priest.

"Chasca denies you the right of sacrifice!" he said, "There is no need. The corn will be saved. The Sun, Raymi, has sent that which will destroy the insects!"

Clearly the Inca was impressed. Bill seemed so sincere. Mr. Whitley was smiling. The three chums were standing erect in poses of confidence.

"Within a day your corn will be on the way to security," Bill said as Mr. Whitley whispered swift words. "Complete your feast and tomorrow you shall see that we speak truth!"

Cliff ran past them all, caught the shrinking, veiled figure and beckoned Caya.

"Go back to our house," he said. "Caya—take her! We've won!"

CHAPTER XVII
FROM BAD TO WORSE

When Cliff returned to his friends he saw that they had been joined by a tall, cold-eyed Indian noble. He and the high priest were exchanging frowning glances: it seemed evident that they disliked each other. Mr. Whitley was whispering hurriedly to Bill. The high priest turned toward Cliff with a sharp word but Bill advanced, held up his hand, and faced the Inca.

"Oh, royal son of the Sun," he began, loudly enough to be heard by many nobles gathered nearby, "Chasca's servant brings report. There was no destruction of your corn by insects, as Huamachaco, your high priest, told you. The corn grew sick because the earth it grows in has become tired and must be made fruitful once more."

"That is not so!" shouted the high priest, forgetting his dignity in his anger.

Bill paid no attention.

"Oh, Inca," he went on, "here, beside me, is one you trust. Is it not so?"

He indicated the new arrival: the Inca glanced at him and smiled. "He is my son, my oldest son," he agreed, "I trust him."

"Make report, oh, son of the Inca," urged Bill.

"Make report," chorused the nobles.

"I make report of this, oh, noble Inca and my father," said the Indian. "This servant of the messenger from the stars came to my fields soon after Chasca appeared among us: he observed the corn and he took up the earth and made magic with it." The crude tests Mr. Whitley had been able to make had seemed to be incantations to the untutored Indian. "Then went he afar among the hills with one of my servants. They came back with something borne in a sack and from that which they brought my servants did make a magic fluid by mixing it with water."

"Their earth is starving for nitrogen," Mr. Whitley said in a low tone to Cliff, "they do not rotate their crops here; that is they plant the same crop until the earth is exhausted, instead of resting it by changing the crop from one sort to another. I brought them some mineral salts rich in nitrogen and saved time by sprinkling the earth around the cornstalks. And we had to make tiny holes in a golden crock to sprinkle with—imagine! A golden sprinkling can."

"Already my corn begins to change and no longer does it droop." The Indian cast a triumphant look at the high priest: evidently there was jealousy. "It was not the insects, as Huamachaco did tell you, oh, my father, but the earth that starved the grain, as I have said to many."

The high priest turned away, but as he did so Cliff, surprised, his eyes bent on himself with a baleful glance. However, he simply stared straight and level at Huamachaco whose eyes shifted aside.

"You have heard," said Bill. "Let the Feast of Raymi go on, and let it be a feast, indeed! When it is finished, all shall divide into bands, some to fetch the magical earth, some to mix the powerful liquid, others to fashion urns with which to make it fall like rain upon the corn, and so, very soon, all of your dying earth will live again and make the corn lift its tassels in joy to Raymi, whose humble messengers we are."

Cliff had not dreamed that Bill could be so glowing in his speech, and he saw that not only the Inca, but his younger son and all of the nobles were impressed. The Inca evidently foresaw trouble between the two men, and rather eagerly he waved his hand toward them all in dismissal.

"Let the feast go on," he said. Then, turning to Cliff, he added: "Think not, oh son of Venus, that I am ungrateful; when the feast to your superior Lord and Master is done with I will give you tokens of my grateful spirit."

Cliff bowed, not quite sure what else to do. Bill, whose middle left finger had again been caressing his ear, until his friends all gave attentions, made a sign again for no speech, and they all allowed themselves to be conducted to places of honor at a special board table, rather crude but lavishly laden with gold and silver dishes, on which were spread a feast of native roast meats, vegetables, a sort of bread made of the maize—only rarely did the Incas make up bread; they used the corn more often in a sort of porridge, or dried and sometimes parched.

"I am glad you came when you did," Cliff told the former history instructor. The others echoed his statement.

"We are not out of the frying pan yet," Bill warned. "Or—if we are, it's most likely because we're about to be dipped into the fire."

"Why?" asked Nicky, thrilling a little with fear and quite a deal more with anticipation of more adventure.

"You saw the priest and the noble glaring at each other?"

They all nodded.

"It was because of their enmity that the noble was so eager to help me," Mr. Whitley stated. "Naturally the chief priest will not like us too well for showing that his judgment was so far wrong."

"But the priest won't dare do anything," Tom volunteered. "The people think we are heroes, don't they?" Bill nodded.

"Just now they do," he agreed. "But—there is no telling—I saw Huamachaco talking to that mysterious stranger as we came—." He paused and suddenly changed his tone, as he added, "Be careful!" and immediately raised his voice again. "Did you ever see so much gold on a table, Chasca, since we left the halls of the dwellers in the skies?"

They saw at once what caused his sudden change. The dark stranger was approaching. By his shifting gaze and the first words he spoke under his breath they knew him to be Sancho Pizzara, the Spaniard who had offered to join them and then had deserted them in the white pass, only to come to grief himself.

"*Buenos di*—Ah, senors!—and you, noble Chasca! Noble Cleeford Gray Chasca!" There was a curl to his lip and Nicky thrust a hand against the table to push himself erect, but Mr. Whitley put a foot against his ankle none too gently in warning as the Spaniard proceeded. "But that is fine, that you shall be Chasca! You can help me."

"You weren't ambushed?" demanded Tom. "We thought——"

"There was some—how you say?—some 'ta-ra-boom-te-ay' in the pass of snow. My men all run away back. Me, I am desert in snow to freeze. But I get here—late. You are already fix up very nice."

"I warned you about the pass," Bill reminded him.

"*Si?*" He dismissed it with a wave of his hand and bent close and motioned to them to listen. "That we shall forget. Now it is to know—is there plenty of gold? But I see it."

"What did you tell these people?" Mr. Whitley demanded. "We heard that you came with some message."

"Tell—? Oh! I tell that I am send by other men of the hills to seek white faces of those who come this way."

"You told them that?" Bill scowled.

"*Si*. But I have not yet tell that you are men I seek."

"No, and you had better not!" said Tom sharply. Bill warned him with a look.

"Why shall I tell that when you can take me to the gold?"

"We are not here for gold," Cliff said evenly. "We told you about my father."

"Then there is that gold for me alone!" smiled Pizarra.

"Do you think we would help you steal it?" asked Cliff very quietly. "If you do, you are wrong. We won't even take away any to pay back Mr. Whitley, because my father's books will make enough to do that. We came here intending to take enough gold away for expenses, but that was before we knew that my father was alive and able to go with us."

"If you go——" said Pizarra, softly, his eyes flashing.

"Do you mean to threaten that you will endanger the life of the man we came here to rescue?" asked Mr. Whitley coldly. "And put these young men in danger?"

"Oh, no," Sancho Pizzara assured him with a shrug. "I am very kind man. Senor el Venus, here, he will guide me safe to the gold. I shall then not put danger to any."

"And—if we refuse?" asked Bill. "Then—will you?"

"Then perhaps I find the white *hombres* hiding under red dye."

"And of course we would sit right still and let him," Nicky could not control his anger. "We wouldn't say he was a disguised Spaniard trying to steal their treasure——" He stopped Cliff had nudged him sharply. But his statement daunted Pizarra. He turned thoughtful. Then he smiled. "There is for you too much danger," he declared. "You will not dare!"

"As surely as you open your mouth——" began Bill.

"If you do, we do!" Tom snapped.

"Tit for tat!" That was Nicky.

"But it cost you nothing to show me where is the gold hide," Pizarra said, rubbing his hands.

"These people have been kind to us," Mr. Whitley said. "We do not like to help you rob them."

"I am mak' friends to his Huamachaco," Pizarra said meaningly. "He is already suspect something."

That was bad, Cliff reflected, then he brightened.

"He has just been discredited by the Inca's son," he stated. "If it came to a test of power——"

"You see what it come to!" Pizarra wheeled and stalked off.

"We ought to——" Mr. Whitley rose; he had in mind the danger to which their move exposed his charges.

"But we can't——" began Cliff.

"He certainly has put us in a tight corner," Bill admitted, "but we can't let him dictate and threaten——"

They followed his staring eyes as he paused. The Inca, his two sons, the high priest and Pizzara were approaching.

"Sit tight," whispered Bill. "Let me do the talking!"

CHAPTER XVIII
TIT FOR TAT

"Certainly you may do the talking," John Whitley agreed to Bill's urgent hint as they all watched the arrival of the other party. "But I cannot understand how Pizzara can dare to risk his own safety——"

"The high priest hates the Inca's older son," Bill answered. "He will be discredited if the corn grows. He would rather see the crop ruined than to have that happen. The Spaniard must guess that. Probably he hinted enough to whet Huamachaco's curiosity. I think the priest might even promise— promise, I said, not give!—him gold for his help in removing us from the scene."

The rest of the party nodded; there was no time for more discussion. The Inca arrived and they all stood up respectfully and bowed to him.

"This man makes a strange story," said the ruler. "He says you come here from across the great blue waters to steal our gold and to take away the white man who is sick."

Bill bowed to the Inca, but his eyes watched the face of the priest; Cliff and his chums saw that the latter was smiling in a satisfied, triumphant way.

"Truly it is a strange tale, oh ruler," Bill spoke without apparent surprise. "A tale that is the more strange because it comes from the lips of one of that race of Spaniards who tore the empire of the Incas to shreds and took much gold away!"

Pizzara snarled as the Inca turned toward him; but he swiftly composed his face to a smile.

"Royal son of the Sun," Pizzara said to the Inca. "Which of us speaks the truth? It is easy to prove. Here come the men!"

Cliff, Nicky and Tom wheeled. There was a commotion among the crowds still mulling around in the great square, drawn by the feeling that something important was happening. Soldiers threw the people aside as they advanced toward the gardens in which the royal table and those for the nobles were set out.

Cliff felt a prickle of fear run along his spine; there was no mistaking the figure coming toward them. It was Huayca, or Whackey, their former mountain guide, the one who had deserted them on the same night that the Spaniard had slipped away. Behind him were two others. They later proved to be the Indian who had accompanied Pizzara to America and the other who had waited in the hills for the quipu from Cuzco.

Soldiers formed a cordon around the garden as though by a previous arrangement; it was as well, for the crowd, sensing one threat in the attitudes of the five strangers, began to murmur and to press in toward the gardens.

"Can you say who these men are?" the Inca demanded, turning to Huayca and signing for him to rise from his posture of kneeling with his face to the ground.

"They are five," replied Huayca. "They have the same height as did five whom I guided toward our trap in the white pass. But their faces are red, the others were white."

"And who, say you, does this man resemble?" Bill indicated Pizzara. "Is he not of the height of a Spaniard who followed us?"

"He is of that height, perhaps," said the former guide. "But him I cannot recognize for I saw him only at a distance."

"But these," he indicated the chums, "they wear robes like those I saw in a pack carried by the men I guided—I could say they are the same robes, noble and great son of the Sun!"

At a word from the second of his associates, soldiers roughly drew Cliff to one side and pushed Nicky and Tom to either side of him.

"Thus they stood in a house in that strange land which I visited," said the other man, and he added, "I recall the picture perfectly and they are of the same height and attitude."

"What say you?" said the Inca, frowning.

"This!" replied Bill, while the chums stood watchful but realizing that he had urged them to let him handle the situation. "This, Inca!" No longer was he humble or quiet. Quipu Bill was stern, erect, his lank figure towering even above that of the tall ruler. "This I answer. White or red—messengers from the sky or visitors from across the blue water—these things do not matter."

He slipped a hand quietly under his robe.

"What does matter is that we came here to save your corn———"

"That is so!" cried the elder son of the Inca, eagerly; he had evidently been waiting for an opportunity to help them.

"Ask this other man what he has come to do," Bill whirled to scowl at Pizzara who cringed instinctively before he could regain his braggadocio pose. "And—further—" went on Bill, "—ask Huamachaco how much gold he has promised to this man for a story that will work against your older son and his friends who seek to save your grain!"

It proved to be a telling thrust; the high priest shifted his eyes and fidgeted under the Inca's inquiring gaze.

"The man speaks wisely," said the younger son, Challcuchima. "Whatever may be their past, my brother has said that his corn begins to thrive again under this servant of Chasca and his magic. And you have seen the high priest's face. I can say truly that my brother has told me before of Huamachaco's envy and fear of him." He had paid Cliff back for sparing him the humiliation of defeat in the wrestling matches. Cliff smiled gratefully and Challcuchima smiled back.

"What magic has this other to match that?" asked the older son quickly using the advantage for his friend, John Whitley, who had shown him how to enrich the earth and help his crop.

Pizzara blustered.

"I do not fling magic about like water," he boasted, "but I will make your corn grow when the fate of these men is settled."

Bill fixed his eye on Pizzara and began to grin; Cliff and his chums relaxed a little. During his conversation Bill had very stealthily and gradually moved toward Cliff; middle finger touching his ear, he had signaled for attention. Cliff was ready, then, when, calling by signal for an answer to his sign-inquiry, "Is anybody coming?" which Bill asked by dropping his right hand to his side with two fingers loosely dangling, Bill stood behind him. Cliff knew that nobody was coming. He knew that Bill knew it. But he knew something else——

"The sign replying 'No!' to any signal is to clasp the two hands lightly behind the back," Cliff thought. "Bill knows no one is coming; he wants my hands behind me." He clasped them.

All that had gone on while Bill was talking and listening. As he turned to pass behind Cliff his hand slipped like lightning from under his robe and Cliff, feeling a cold object, found his hands clasped around a small automatic revolver.

"Keep it behind you," muttered Bill, and then moved on and went close to the Inca. From where he had been standing, beside the other end of the rude table, his move to get closer to the ruler seemed quite natural. "Clever Bill," thought Cliff, "to make me put my hands behind me to get this revolver, by using the Mystery Boys' sign. I wonder why he gave me the weapon?"

"Oh, Senor Pizzara," Bill threw over his shoulder. "So you have magic, have you?" He faced the ruler. "Inca," he said, "noble Son of the Sun, this man says he has magic. Shall we have a test of his power compared to that of Chasca, Page of the Sun?"

That pleased the entire group. The Indians were always eager to see any marvels. Bill's plan was clearer to Cliff but he held the revolver behind him, although several soldiers saw the glinting object and stepped forward, then hesitated and drew back at Bill's words. They had not actually seen the weapon pass from Bill to Cliff, and they were not sure that it had done so. They waited to see what would happen.

"Let this man show his magic to Chasca!" snapped Bill.

They all chorused, "Let him show his magic!"

Pizzara grimaced at Bill and turned to the Inca.

"I fear to show my magic," he said. "It is too powerful——"

"He has none," Bill cried, then whirled toward Huamachaco. "Let your high priest show his magic, then."

But apparently the high priest still had some fear that the young fellow with the bright and flowing locks might be truly a messenger from the skies. He backed away, frowning, shaking his head. "It is not good to show my magic to the ones who are not in the sacred order," he muttered.

"What? No magic? Yet Chasca can show some! Chasca—oh, Inca, take from the youth of the skies that which he offers."

The Inca turned, gazing in surprise as did all the Peruvians, as Cliff produced the revolver. "The safety catch is on," Bill murmured. "Let him have it, Cliff."

The Inca took the glittering steel object gingerly, awed by it. He examined it while the others stared, but kept at a safe distance. Pizzara began to skulk away but soldiers stopped him.

"Point it—so!" suggested Bill, showing the ruler how to direct the muzzle in the general direction of Pizzara's stomach.

"No! No!" cried the man, groveling and pushing a soldier in front of his own person.

"Bring him back!" snapped the Inca and the soldiers pushed Pizzara forward.

"Pull on that little stick," Bill suggested. The safety catch prevented the Inca from discharging the weapon but the effect of Bill's words upon Pizzara was amusing; he fell on the ground and tried to crawl behind Challcuchima.

"Nothing happens and yet the man who can save your corn is a worm, crawling about, just because of our magic," said Bill. He took the weapon which the Inca was very glad to relinquish.

"Get up!" Bill said curtly. Pizzara stood cringing.

"Say to the Inca—is what you told Huamachaco the truth?" The muzzle slipped upward along Pizzara's buttons and he knew there was an expert hand releasing the safety catch.

"No! No!" he shouted. "Inca, it was not so."

"Take him away!" the Inca signed to the soldiers and for the time the danger was past.

No one interfered as, leaving the table, the five friends went quickly to their retreat in the Star Temple.

"We must change our plans," Bill said, swiftly when they were alone. "We must get together all our things that we will need—the things Cliff suggested bringing may come in handy after all!—and I will bring comrade Cliff's pa tonight and we will make a try for that ledge where our rope is hidden."

"What is it, Caya?" Cliff asked as the girl came to fall on her knees before him. He signed for her to rise.

"Use your magic to return to the skies," she begged. "They talked after you went. I went near. I heard. They let you show them the magic for the corn and then the high priest says he can make greater magic to destroy you!"

Cliff whispered to Mr. Whitley and Bill, then in his slow quichua he said to the trembling girl: "We are not from the stars, Caya. We are here to save my father, the pale man who has been a prisoner for so long."

The girl clasped her hands and stared. Slowly his words penetrated her understanding.

"Oh!" she gasped. "See then—! I can help! You saved my sister! I will help you—save you and your father also if it shall please Raymi that one so humble shall do so much!"

"How?" asked Tom, always practical.

"There is a secret way—it is not known to me, but I shall learn from one who knows!"

"We saved her sister and now she will save us," Nicky exulted. "The Spaniard queered us"—he was so excited he used slang, but they did not notice. "We paid him back. Just as I said."

"Yes," said Cliff. "It's 'tit for tat' all around!"

CHAPTER XIX
HUAMACHACO'S SECRET

"How can you find out about the secret pass if you don't know already?" asked Tom.

"Don't be too inquisitive," reproved Mr. Whitley. "If she can find out that is enough for us."

"But in trying to find out she might blunder," Tom urged. "Huamachaco, for example, might grow suspicious and watch us all."

"I tell you my way," she said eagerly. "I do not make danger. In the mountains are great herds of vicuna—small cattle—sheep."

"And you know one of the shepherds?" Cliff saw the truth.

Caya looked down bashfully "Yes." She was shy as she spoke. "One comes at night. We walk and talk. Late tonight I will come to you and I will know the way."

They glanced at one another dubiously.

"'Late tonight' won't be too late, will it?" Tom wondered.

"They won't disturb us until they learn what I used on the corn field," Mr. Whitley said. "We surely have the rest of the day and the coming night, because they must finish the feast."

"That makes you safe," Bill said. "I guess the rest of us can stay quiet and keep out of mischief." If he said mischief they all knew that he meant "danger."

Caya hurried away and the others busied themselves getting their few necessary belongings together. Caya's plan was that when they went, late at night, she could lead them to the pass where she knew her influence over her young shepherd sweetheart would enable her to find the way. Then they could hide until she could bring enough food to sustain them after she said farewell in the mountains. Perhaps her shepherd might even be induced to feed them; she would see what he would do. She was sure he would come to see her that evening.

She slipped away to help serve at the feast which was still progressing, and to linger near the tables of the nobles to learn anything she could about their plans.

"If she doesn't come back we can probably get to our ledge, and escape that way," Nicky suggested.

"I think that way is closed," Bill said. "Pizzara came that way: from the top of the ledge he probably discovered the twine and he may have used the same scheme to get down. But I don't think he was brainy enough to hide the twine—and he could not get up high enough to do that. We had to make our human ladder, you remember, to get the twine end out of sight."

"We will have to depend upon Caya," said Mr. Whitley. "And I only hope one thing—that her shepherd friend keeps his regular tryst with her."

"We won't take these back, will we?" asked Nicky, holding up a handful of thin sticks about ten inches long, heavily crusted for most of their length with fat grayish stuff.

"We can slip them into our robes," Mr. Whitley said. "They are only colored lights, red, blue and green, but they might be useful as torches and they burn a long time."

"We were going to use them if we had to pretend to make a display of magic, weren't we?" asked Nicky who had not been fully aware of the plan Cliff had originally made. That plan had been to come into the valley as strangers, wanderers, Indians from a distant place, and then, if necessary, to use simple colored lights and other things to impress the Inca's subjects.

The plan had been changed by the fact that Cliff's hair came out of his dye-bath a vivid golden red; he was posing as Chasca, the youth of the bright and flowing locks and the fireworks had not been needed since they burned red fire on the ledge.

"How about these?" asked Cliff, picking up some squat, stubby paper tubes. But no one answered. Huamachaco had entered the main temple and was approaching slowly. Cliff mechanically dropped his hand into an inside pocket sewed inside the robe by Bill. He forgot his question in the sudden suspicion brought into his mind by the arrival of their enemy.

But Huamachaco seemed to be no enemy; he was smiling. He was sorry that he had listened to the stranger's false tale, he said, and the Inca wished to show them honor and to ask the noble Chasca to forgive his suspicion. Would they not join the Inca at the feast?

To refuse might bring on the Inca's anger; it was not wise to slight him. They agreed to go and followed Huamachaco to the main door of the temple. He drew back and stepped aside, motioning to Cliff. "Hailli, Chasca!" cried someone from beyond the doorway and as Bill nudged him Cliff stepped out.

Then he stared, grew tense and his blood froze.

The Inca, Challcuchima and the others, as well as Pizzara, standing at one side, he scarcely noticed. His eyes flew to a group of soldiers. They were dragging a man's limp figure! The man wore European clothes, though ragged ones; his face was white! With a scream Cliff sprang forward.

"Father!" he cried, and again, "Father!"

"You see!" cried Sancho Pizzara to Huamachaco, "I told truth!"

"Take him under guard!" growled the Inca. Cliff was trapped.

CHAPTER XX
ON THE TEMPLE STEPS

There was an instant of absolute silence. Cliff was hesitating over the chance of springing past the soldiers to get to his father. The friends behind were stunned. The soldiers still had enough awe of "Chasca" to delay.

Then Huamachaco caught one of Cliff's arms and dragged him sharply down the steps and sideways so that he stumbled. Challcuchima caught him as he scuffled down the stone slabs, off his balance. In the same second Tom and Nicky had leaped past Bill. Nicky grappled with and tripped the Indian priest while Tom dragged down Challcuchima from behind. Bill and Mr. Whitley were out on the steps at once. Bill lifted the shining revolver which he had recovered from Cliff when they left the feast.

"Stop!" he shouted. But there was a grumble and murmur from the crowd pressed against the line of soldiers, with their tin-and-copper alloy swords out and ready. There was more danger than merely that of arrest and confinement. There was an ominous threat in the sound of that hoarsely guttural murmur.

Cliff had his arms free; a soldier, seeing that no harm came to those who had seized Chasca, himself advanced. Cliff backed toward the temple steps again, at Mr. Whitley's swift order.

But Challcuchima had flung off Tom, had, in fact, given him a vicious punch that took Tom's wind for the instant.

Challcuchima caught at Cliff again. Cliff's hand shot out as Mr. Whitley leaped off the step and swung the Inca's older brother aside before he could aid Challcuchima. Cliff's blow struck true and the younger son went down.

"Get back into the temple!" cried Bill.

There was a sharp, startling bark from his revolver; he fired above the heads of the crowd.

That unusual sound arrested every motion for an instant. Nicky squirmed free from Huamachaco who had risen and grasped him. Cliff started backward but his foot caught on the lowest step. He lost his balance but Nicky caught and steadied him. Bill and Mr. Whitley rushed down to aid Tom, who had dropped, sick and weakened by Challcuchima's unexpected blow.

Then there came an ominous sound—a laugh of triumph.

The Inca, with several soldiers, had gained the top step and escape into the temple was cut off!

The angry crowd surged forward, pushing the soldiers with them.

Cliff leaped forward and caught Tom, steadying him as he regained his breath. Bill swung and pointed his weapon straight at the Inca.

"You get back," he said meaningly in quichua, "or this magic stick will speak and send you to your fathers!"

The Inca wavered uncertainly; but Challcuchima thrust between Cliff and Tom, Nicky raced to his assistance, Huamachaco cried out, "Capture the one who calls a white stranger his father!" and the entire crowd surged forward.

Bill and Mr. Whitley leaped up on the steps in concerted action and so sudden and unexpected was the rush that they upset one soldier who clutched at his comrade. Both fell. Bill gave the Inca a poke and he tottered down the side steps.

But others were ready to rush in.

Cliff spoke swiftly to his comrades, drew a paper of matches from his pocket; the crowd hesitated as he struck a match, backed to the cleared space behind them that offered a way to the temple steps. The soldiers had not yet closed in behind them.

Cliff did not speak; but his upflung hand caused curiosity in the minds of the simple natives.

Even the soldiers held quiet, an officer muttering some word to stay them. Methodically Cliff drew a squat, stubby paper tube from his robe. He handed it to Nicky; another to Tom.

"Light the fuses when I strike the match," he whispered. "Then throw them down in front of us and all make for the doorway!"

He drew out a third tube, struck a match. Three fuses came together. But at the same instant a soldier leaped forward to jostle Cliff's arm. But the fuses caught.

Their sputter heralded a trickle of pitchy, pungent black smoke; the tubes were such smoke-pots as are used by motion picture companies, and such as were used in the war, for fire scenes and smoke screens.

"Drop them—now!" cried Cliff. The three flung down their tubes and retreated; Bill and Mr. Whitley were at the door. Cliff lit another tube as Mr. Whitley reached to hasten the youths up the steps.

The crowd, seeing them move back a step, began to surge forward but the smoke began to pour up in a huge, spreading cloud. It spread in the slight breeze, blew into the eyes and throats of the soldiers and of the mob.

Coughing, choking, startled and awed, they fell back against those pressing forward. The smoke spread into a great fan, hiding the exit of the five; the only one who might have seen them was the Inca; but he was too busy picking himself up.

The smoke subsided. The crowd gasped.

Their quarry seemed to have disappeared as if by magic!

CHAPTER XXI
RATS IN A TRAP

"You meant well," Bill panted, as they retreated into their antechamber. "Cliff, it was a splendid idea that you had. But——"

"With no door to barricade, we are no better off," Cliff admitted. "They will soon discover that we came in here."

"We are like rats in a trap!" said Tom. "Bill, next time you shoot off that pistol you will have to aim lower—or we will have to give up."

"If there was some place to hide," said Nicky despairingly.

"But there isn't," said Cliff. "I forgot that the temple had no door."

"There they come!" whispered Tom.

They heard cautious feet tramping up the temple steps and looked around desperately.

Cliff snatched up a golden platter and drew back his arm. But Mr. Whitley caught his hand, and turned to watch a huge tapestry swinging with a curious motion on the inner wall of the anteroom.

Cliff faced that way as did all of his companions. Were they to be attacked from behind that curtain?

The side of the hanging cloth shook and then they saw Caya! Swiftly, with one finger to her lip, she beckoned. In an instant, not even stopping for their belongings, the five moved on tip-toe to the place where she stood.

Wordlessly they trusted themselves behind that curtain, going into the unknown.

There was another doorway there, concealed by the hanging; they had never thought of looking behind that; there were so many decorative cloths hung upon the wall as backgrounds for ornaments and to soften the harsh appearance of rough stone that no other purpose had occurred to them.

Nevertheless, the tapestry screened a way out!

In darkness, following Caya with no more sound than they were compelled to make, they gave each other whispered directions as Cliff, in the lead, felt her steady him at the edge of a downward step.

"It's stairs," Cliff whispered.

"To the tunnels!" Tom guessed.

Slowly, carefully, down they went. Faintly through the opening, muffled by the hanging, they heard shouts of baffled rage; the soldiers and the people had forgotten their reverence for the supposedly sacred temple, for if the priests had come in alone they would have sought the way to the tunnels at once.

At the foot of the stairs, down about thirty steps, Caya whispered, her lips close to Cliff's ear.

"I take you to your white father."

In a time that seemed an age, feeling their way through the darkness, they came to a point where she urged them to wait for her. She would bring Cliff's father if there was a chance.

In silence, shivering a little from sheer nervous strain, the five waited, not daring to light the several pocket flashlights they had, even for an instant. They listened with quaking forms to every tiny sound; was that a stealthy step—or the drip of water—or a rat? They did not know. They dared not try to see.

After a long wait a soft gliding sound reached them; they were alert, listening, straining their ears. Caya's voice reassured them but her news instantly awakened fear again.

"They are coming!" she whispered to Bill. "I did find the white man alone while his guards take counsel with messengers. I stand where white man sees. I do so—" she made a beckoning motion. "He follow. But others are near. I must lead them away while you escape. Go, straight forward. Do not turn. You will come to a room full of gold and silver. At its side are steps. They go into the Temple of the Sun."

She paused. Far away they could hear shouts.

"Go there," she resumed. "None dares to enter the Temple of the Sun except the Inca, his Coya"—the queen—"and the high priest. They will not think to seek there. Go, quickly!"

"But where are you going?" asked Cliff.

"To lead the soldiers another way while you escape."

"We can't let you do that!" cried the boy; and his chums, with one accord, echoed it. But the brave girl had already turned and glided away.

"Nothing else for it," whispered Bill. "Come on—to the Sun Temple!"

While they ran they heard shouts in the distance, and then a high, shrill scream!

Cliff gritted his teeth.

"If you'd let me go back and get her——"

But they would not.

CHAPTER XXII
THE TEMPLE OF THE SUN

Never before had Nicky, Tom, or the older men, seen so much treasure as they found at the end of the passage. Cliff had seen the great room filled with gold and precious cloths and metals once before, when the king's son took him there to inquire about the statuette.

"Where can Caya have left my father?" Cliff said anxiously when he had taken a swift glance around the treasure room; his chums almost forgot their danger, so awed and fascinated were they.

But Mr. Whitley hurried them all to the steps and up them.

The stairway into the ante-room, or rear portion of the Sun Temple were not straight; they curved like steps in a lighthouse tower.

At their top, emerging after spying carefully, the fugitives found themselves in a narrow room, a sort of Priests' room, running across the back of the edifice, behind the huge placque on which was embossed and enscrolled the massive face with the Sun-rays around it. Therefore the rear room had two doorways, one on each side of the placque, looking into the main temple. Great tapestries screened these doorways. Bill lost no time in spying through into the main room; finding that deserted, he nodded and permitted the others to ascend into the back room, forbidding loud words in case anyone came into the front temple room by chance, though few had the privilege of entry there.

As they entered, single file, they all grew tense again—it seemed that they were betrayed! A huge curtain hung on the wall opposite to the doorways began to quiver.

Bill hurriedly produced his weapon. "Come forth!" he muttered in quichua; the curtain remained without further stir.

"Look out!" gasped Nicky, "he might have a bow'n arrow!"

Of course he spoke in English, and at the sound of the words there came a low whisper.

"Do not fire!"

From behind the curtain emerged a white man!

"Father!" gasped Cliff, forgetting all cautions. He and his father, so long separated, were at last rejoined.

Their meeting was joyful; but Cliff lost no time in presenting the gray-haired, weak old scholar to the others—except Bill, who had already visited Mr. Gray.

They were not left long without interruption, but, fortunately, when the tension of a steady step ascending the curved stairs was almost unendurable, a lithe, young soldier, hardly older than the chums, made his appearance, stopping before he reached the top step. He carried a short throwing spear, with its point toward himself, a token of his errand being peaceful.

He explained hurriedly that he was Caya's older brother, belonging to the Palace guard of picked youths, a sort of picked reserve regiment, called out on occasions such as this.

They liked him at once; but they respected his refusal to come into the Temple. "It is forbidden!" he said, simply, to Bill, and told his story briefly from the steps.

Caya had been caught; she had managed to see him. She sent him to search for the white man, and then, if he found him, to convey him to the temple steps and bid him go up. But Mr. Gray, once free, had come there already.

"I go, then, to my duty," said the young soldier. "Because you saved my sister—from—the sacrifice—and she is very dear to me, for we are twins!— I will try to save your lives tonight."

"Do you know the secret way?" asked Bill. "So we can get out of the valley?"

The soldier shook his head.

"No. But I will ask to have 'leave.' I will pretend to be seeking for you—I hope I shall get to the hill path by following some soldiers secretly despatched to duty by a High Priest."

"Yes," Tom agreed. "He would know the secret ways and might send soldiers to guard them."

But when they asked the young soldier about Caya, his sister, he became very sad.

"She is a captive," he told Bill, who interpreted. "There is nothing that can be done. Even I, in the Inca's junior guard, cannot see her."

"Who can?" demanded Nicky.

"The Inca alone," said the youthful brother.

He went down the stairway, promising to return after dark, if opportunity permitted. He was certain that they would not be molested because the ceremonies in the temple were finished and the feasting would continue as soon as the disturbance was ended.

"I think," Nicky suggested, after the soldier went, "we ought to try to help Caya."

"So do I!" declared Cliff and Tom echoed the fact that she had given up her liberty for their sakes. Cliff suggested a plan and although they hesitated at first, Mr. Whitley, Mr. Gray and Bill finally agreed to it.

Then they began, as is so often the case, to become enthusiastic and hopeful, and also added ideas of their own.

"We would need Tom, too," Mr. Whitley hesitated.

"I'm not afraid," Tom said. "If I can do anything to help! Tell me what it is."

"We must get that rope that we hid at the ledge," Bill told him. "My idea is for you to strip down to the sort of costume the Inca's 'chasquis' or messengers, wear. I am going to make up a quipu like one that would be used to identify the Inca's runners, and you are to take it and go to the place we left our rope, for we will need it in the mountain passes. If you meet anybody you can show the quipu and they won't stop you. If you meet soldiers near the ledge, show the quipu and say 'I go to get what the Inca has learned about.' Then, even if they go with you they won't take the rope away."

"Can't I go, too?" Nicky pleaded. "The chances would be better with two——"

"Oh, no," Mr. Whitley decided. "Tom proved that he can run during the races, and—I must say this in frankness, Nicky—he can keep a quiet tongue and a level head if an emergency comes before him."

Nicky was crestfallen, but had he been able to look into the future he would not have been depressed at his forced inactivity just for the time.

Tom rehearsed his quichua words, Cliff went over, again and again, the things he might be called on to do and to say. Bill, Mr. Gray and their leader revised and discussed their plan until they could see no possible emergency that could come up that they would not be prepared to meet.

With his fading flashlight, later replaced by Mr. Whitley's, Bill fashioned a simple quipu of woven strands, taken from a raveled edge of a woolen wall hanging: he knotted it craftily.

CHAPTER XXIII
CHASCA APPEARS AGAIN

Nothing happened to disturb the quiet of the old temple during the afternoon. The early feasting had been completed and, except for some soldiers whom a priest, evidently not quite convinced of miracles, was exhorting to find the vanished ones, all was quiet.

Soon after dark Tom slipped out into the deserted square, on his way to secure the rope.

Not long after that Cliff and Bill started on their mission.

The Inca was in his palace, the low building at one side of the public square: he was tired and worried.

Cliff, who remembered the way from the Palace to the treasure room, led Bill, counting the turns, for he had been observant by habit and had a retentive memory.

The Inca, listening to the conclusion of a report from one of his palace guards, turned back as the man went away. To his amazement he looked into that magic stick which, earlier in the day, he had held while the Spaniard groveled. Now its magic had turned on him. Thus he thought about Bill's revolver.

Behind him in the passage, concealed by curtains, heavy and closely woven, Cliff made ready his part of the little tableau that was to follow. Their plan was to awe the Inca, perhaps to terrify him. They had tried to foresee every possible chance that could come up. As Bill held his "magic stick" he spoke. He used no quichua, but spoke the secret tongue of the nobles.

"A silent tongue lives long, O, Inca!" he said. "Call not!"

"Servant of Chasca," the Inca used the same speech, "How came thy form to my palace? Or art thou Cupay?"—that was the Inca tribe word for an evil spirit.

"I come, thou who sayest thou art royal son of the Sun and who dost seek to destroy that other more royal one, Chasca. Can he be destroyed? Ask of thy son, Challcuchima, who strove with him and made a bargain that he might not go down in defeat—and then, like thy own evil self, did break his word to the youth of the bright and flowing locks!"

The Inca was a brave man but he hesitated between his desire to call out and his superstitious fear.

"Thou Inca—earth flesh and not from the skies—to the truth that Raymi is merciful and his messenger is even the same thou dost owe thy life. Look!"

As he spoke the last word in a low, sharp voice, Bill drew aside the hangings. Cliff had wedged a colored-fire stick in a crack of the stones of the corridor: at the approach of the agreed signal he struck a match and ignited it: it flared up in a vivid, weird green that lighted up the space brilliantly. Cliff quickly assumed a posture with arms folded, the light behind him picking out his glowing hair and coloring it strangely.

No wonder the Inca cringed: he had built up a cult of belief that now claimed his own mind. He fell back a step.

"Say on, Chasca!" said Bill, ("And make it quick!" he added in English).

Cliff spoke the lines he had practiced all afternoon.

"Inca," he said in quichua, "twice today you have tried to slay. Raymi does not wish a sacrifice. I am sent to save your corn. Release, then, Caya—or my wrath shall smite!"

Bill saw that the short, green color-fire must go out. He dropped the curtain swiftly just as it did so. Cliff, aware of his part, snatched the wooden butt from its place and retired to the steps, out of sight.

"Chasca——" began the Inca.

"You speak too late!" Bill declared, again snatching away the concealing drapery. The Inca's eyes bulged. Gone was the light and the bright-haired figure.

He stammered and gulped.

"Answer to me and Chasca will hear," Bill said. "Say quickly, do you as Chasca commands?"

But a crafty light was in the Indian's eyes.

"Let Chasca appear while the curtain is open," he said.

In English Bill spoke to Cliff. What he said was not understood by the Inca, but it told Cliff they must use the second part of their plan—an emergency had arisen. Bill lifted a hand, calling, "Behold!" but as he did so, attracting the Inca's eyes toward the curtains, he stepped back a pace. The curtain dropped. Instantly, suspecting a trap, the Inca whirled to face Bill—just as Bill had desired, for at that instant Cliff, who had thus been given time to reach the hanging, flung it aside and leaped upon the Indian from behind as Bill, with a simultaneous leap, flung a hand over the royal mouth.

Struggling, the Inca went down: the surprise helped them. Soon he was gagged with an end of the turban or llantu, the woven wool head dress which he wore when not covered by the crimson or scarlet borla. With an end of the long cloth they hastily cut bindings for hands and ankles. And not too soon.

Across the square came the measured tramp of many feet!

"Will you have time?" asked Cliff, breathlessly.

"I hope so."

Bill ruthlessly stripped off the borla from the Inca's head, snatched off his robe of state, and with Cliff's help made hurried disposal of the inert and helpless body.

"Just in time——" Cliff whispered. "They are here."

The tramping stopped suddenly at a sharp command. With only a brief delay to remove his sandals, an officer came into the doorway.

"O, royal son of the Sun," he said, after he had bowed his head low in respect.

He looked around. On a stool on the side of the room far away from the single lamp, what looked to him like the form of the Inca bent over some turbans which he seemed to be sorting on a low bench over which the gaudy colored woolen and spun vicuna-fleece hung in thick folds.

There was no other in the room. Cliff had fled behind the curtain.

"Say on," came a mutter.

"We have caught one of the servants of Chasca," reported the soldier.

The form bent over the turban material straightened but only half turned.

"It is the one that Chasca called—'Nee-kee!'"

CHAPTER XXIV
THE INCA SPEAKS

Cliff, hiding in the tunnel stairway, heard the last speech and his hands clenched. Nicky was a captive!

He could not see and dared not show himself to get nearer: he must stay as he was and trust to Bill, masquerading as the Inca, to solve this really unexpected problem. They had gone over everything so carefully! There had not been a single point, possibility or chance that they had not covered—except this one!

They had instructed Nicky: they had made their own plans. But that Nicky should be brought to the Inca had not occurred to them.

How would Bill handle it?

If Nicky were brought in would he recognize Bill, or cause suspicion in the soldier's mind by his look?

And Cliff could not see! He must hide.

"You are a good soldier," Bill spoke as nearly as he could in the tones of the Inca. "I shall not forget your zeal. Let the servant of Chasca be set before me."

There was an order, a commotion, and Nicky stood before him. How had he been captured? Then were the two older companions also captives? How could Bill discover the facts?

"Was he alone caught?" asked Bill, as the Inca.

"Oh light of the day, yes."

Then the others might still be safe!

"I thought to seek once more through the tunnels," explained the soldier. "I went with my men. Coming to the room beneath the great and holy Temple, Corrichanca——" the place of gold, or the greatest, holiest of the temples——"I thought there was a sound. I sought behind every tapestry and under piles of rich golden cloth—may Raymi forgive me that I did touch them with my poor hands!—and this Nee-kee did hide."

Much later Nicky explained to his chums that he had crept down the stone stairway to watch for any possible hint of the return of his friends and then had been attracted by the gold and had been caught by the unexpectedly quiet approach of the soldier.

Nicky knew, or suspected at least, that the figure over in the shadows was his own friend, Bill. But he was, for once, master of his face: he did not betray his thoughts. He kept perfectly still, standing between two soldiers.

Cliff, in hiding, wondered what Bill could do, what he would say.

"Are soldiers now in the secret ways?" asked Bill.

"No, most powerful ray of the Sun's light on earth," replied the captain. "The search was completed when I discovered this one: no other could be found."

"And yet," and Bill raised his voice, determined that it must carry information to Cliff so that he could guide his own future by what he heard. "And yet we may find even Chasca in that tunnel unless he runs very fast. It comes to me as a prophecy that he may be near to liberate his servant. But if so, no doubt he will run away or disappear."

Cliff, listening, heard that and determined that he would run very fast and get back to his father and Mr. Whitley and tell them what had happened, so that they would not go down to look for Nicky. But he hesitated. Perhaps Bill had more instructions for him!

Cliff crept a little way down the corridor, to be able to catch distinctly every word of Bill's next speech, given in quichua.

"I must go to the dungeons. I will speak with Caya. She must be made to tell all. I take Nee-kee with me. Soldier, guard this palace—let no one enter here. The guards at the dungeon will help me take Caya to the temple, Corrichanca, of the god, Raymi, where, in front of those white ones in their dyed skins, she shall tell me the truth."

Bill thus gave Cliff all the information he needed. Down the steps and back to the Sun Temple sped Cliff, quite sure of his way.

He identified himself to the watchful father, Mr. Whitley also, and explained breathlessly what had happened and what Bill had told him he would do. They must wait, they decided.

But where was Tom. Would he get the rope? Would he be caught?

And while they debated, in the palace the Coya, or queen, entered the audience room from another chamber. She looked around. Something strange about the pile of wool in the corner attracted her attention. Bill had already gone. But the queen saw the real Inca.

"Ho—guards!—hither!" she cried. "Help me! The Inca is bound beneath these wools!"

CHAPTER XXV
TOM'S ADVENTURE

Tom did not go very far on his way before he saw a small troop of soldiers guarding the road.

He hesitated: if he tried to slip around them he might run into others: if he ran boldly past them it would test his nerve but it was really the safest course.

He kept on, running lightly, drawing his breath a little faster than usual, more from excitement than from weariness.

"Stop, chasqui!" commanded the officer in charge as Tom ran close to the resting soldiers. "Where run you so fast?"

Tom showed the quipu Bill had made up.

"I run for the Inca," he said.

The officer studied his face: while the light was only that coming from the stars he peered closely.

"I do not know you," he declared.

Tom drew himself up to his full height. He stared at the officer, trying to be haughty.

The officer was not impressed. At the same time, he did not quite dare to delay a messenger with the royal proof, the quipu that seemed to indicate Tom's errand as genuine.

He did not release the grip he had taken on Tom's arm.

A soldier stepped forward and made a salute.

"Let me run with the chasqui," he said. "Thus the Inca's message will not be delayed and if the fellow is carrying the royal token without warrant I can bring him back."

This did not suit Tom but he said nothing. It flashed through his mind that this was no time to raise a disturbance: later on he might think of some way to elude the soldier.

"See that you do," said the officer. Tom whirled, snatched his arm free and ran. The soldier ran as lightly, as swiftly as he.

Tom had been in the races during the ceremonies of naming Challcuchima successor to the Inca's rule: it suited his present purpose to make the soldier at his side run his best, to tire him quickly.

But, as the road was spurned by his light feet, he realized that the soldier was not one to tire quickly: step for step, with easy breath and unwearied muscles, he kept the pace. Then Tom received a surprise.

They were passing the outskirts of the city of Quichaka and had come to a small house; it was not of the splendid stone, matched and sturdy, that marked the noble palaces; it was built of the sticky earth mixed with rushes or reeds and grasses, of which the Peruvians made bricks to use in their homes for the more humble people.

"Turn with me," said the soldier.

Tom hesitated. What was the fellow's purpose? He saw that his companion was young, but he had not recognized him.

But, as they came into the dimly lit room wherein an aged couple squatted, he stared.

His soldier companion was Caya's brother!

The youth wasted little time explaining to his parents: the woman began to mutter: she was afraid of what could happen if they shielded these lads from the world beyond their mountains. But the youth's father was different: he understood his son's explanation readily and nodded. The soldier told Tom to remain there when Tom had explained his errand.

"There is no need to run so far," he said. "I will find a rope that will be strong and light."

"It will save time," Tom said.

"Yes—and time is precious!"

The old man listened. Finally he spoke.

"What of Caya?"

"I think she is safe," Tom told him, and in what quichua he could master, aided by signs, he detailed what he knew of the plan to save her. The old woman was horrified at what she understood of the plan to go to the Inca, but the man laughed with a hoarse, hearty chuckle.

"Shame!" cried his old wife. "That you laugh at the son of the Sun."

"But he has brought it upon himself," the man assured her. "If he were a true descendant of the old line of rulers I would not dare to laugh: but you know he is not of the true line and when we of his council advised him to free the white stranger who would, I think, write in his papers but not tell others how to find us, he refused. This is therefore his punishment for being vain of his own counsel!"

Meanwhile Tom and the young soldier discussed plans. The latter was certain that Caya's shepherd would never be able to come to see her tonight: the secret ways were all guarded by many soldiers and the hills were full of the searching natives.

"But there is a way, I think," he said. "I know of an old aqueduct that has not been filled with water for years. It was built to take water to flood the secret tunnels if any came to steal our treasure; but most people, I believe, forget what it is for and how to operate its old water gate. Stay you here until I look at the gate to be sure it is not open and that we can get into its deep bed: also I will hide a strong rope there and come back. Then we will get your friends. Caya, if she is free, must leave the city. I think the mother of her shepherd in the hills will care for her until the Inca has forgotten."

He hurried away and Tom, resting and waiting, wondering what was happening and how his comrades fared, listened to much that would have been interesting under other circumstances.

The old man told him the history of the hidden valley: told how the race began, for he was a student and a quipucamaya, or reader of the records, and knew much of the legend and history: but while Tom listened respectfully, his mind was far away.

He was glad when the young soldier came back.

He had all in readiness and after thanking the older people and being assured by the man that he would get bundles of food ready so that they could be picked up by his son later, Tom and his companion set out for the city, going in ways that took them safely past all guards.

But when they reached the square they stopped. A crowd was clamoring and shouting outside the Temple to the Sun and it was easy to tell that their angry shouts meant dire danger for the persons who might be within its walls.

And Tom did not know who was there, or what to do!

CHAPTER XXVI
INTO THE DUNGEONS

Within the rear chamber of the Sun Temple Cliff, his father and Mr. Whitley heard the roar of the furious people. The Coya had discovered her husband, the Inca, and soldiers had released him: from them the news had spread swiftly among the populace. The chief priest and other nobles had been summoned.

In the passages Bill and Nicky finally reached the golden room, ignorant of this failure of all their carefully laid plans.

In the square Tom, with Caya's brother, saw the procession going toward the Sun Temple. Only the Inca and his highest priests had the privilege of entering there—and they were going in!

"There is but one place we have not sought," Huamachaco had said. "That temple so sacred! Those men and youths with dyed skins, as the Spaniard has told us—they would profane its very sanctuary with their vile presence. Come—you shall see!"

Tom proposed, in his halting quichua, that he and Caya's brother press through the throng; but the young soldier had a better plan. "No," he said. "I have learned the way. We go to the lower level from the Inca's palace—even that I dare for you!—and then we shall see if the way is clear to the old water way. I will wait there and you shall bring your friends. Come. I show the way."

The palace was deserted: all minds and all eyes were focused on the temple.

"Let's lose no time!" whispered Tom, and the two youths made all the haste they could. They were already in the passages when from the mob around the Sun Temple came a deep, throaty roar—the throaty, deep lust-cry of a mob thirsting for vengeance for a seeming insult to their temple!

The Inca had gone in with his aide and then had hurried to the doorway again to signal that they had found their prey.

At the foot of the steps in the treasure room Bill sent Nicky up to tell his friends to be ready, to see if Cliff had returned to them safely and to learn what they knew of Tom.

Nicky walked up the steps, cautiously, and found himself facing the Inca and his chief priest and the Spaniard. In their fury the nobles had overlooked the insult of the Spaniard's entry into the sacred chamber.

Nicky saw at once that he had blundered into a trap. John Whitley, Mr. Gray, and Cliff faced the angry noble and the Inca, desperately, not knowing what to do. The crowd in the square gave them no chance to escape that way. They could not know that the passages were not already invaded by soldiers. Indeed, there were detachments already coming from the palace.

Far away down a lateral passageway Caya's brother showed Tom the place where, when the tunnels were made, an opening had been left into an old waterway; in case of menace to the treasures, a former Inca had provided a way to flood the tunnels.

The young soldier began as quietly as he could to tear away the old debris that had collected, while Tom hurried back along the tunnel, making careful note of the way, planning to tell his friends to hurry, that the way for escape was found!

At the foot of the steps he found Bill.

"Something has gone wrong!" Bill whispered. "Nicky went up the steps five minutes since. He hasn't come down. I haven't heard from anybody. But I think I hear sounds in the tunnels. Don't you?"

Tom listened.

"Yes, I do," he said, under his breath. "Bill, I'll slip up the stairs—and see what's what!"

"Too late!" Bill whispered.

Far away down the passages came shouts. Once they saw a light flash. They were being cornered, surrounded. If there was no way from the temple they were helpless.

Tom told his story in hurried words.

Yet the news had come too late, it seemed. Unless quick thinking could get them out of the toils, they were doomed.

Up above, in the temple, the Inca was delivering his words of doom. "You can no longer be free!" he said sharply. "Escape is not possible. You have profaned our temples! You have deceived us! You shall go to the dungeons."

Cliff looked from one to the other of his friends. If only Tom was there—he knew from Nicky where Bill was!—they could make one desperate effort! Perhaps they might use his remaining smoke pot. But Tom was not there!

Nicky gripped his arm.

From the lower levels came a muffled report! Bill had fired into the air as a body of soldiers came, in their light cotton quilted armor, carrying bows and arrows and short spears; they had to stop in face of his "magic stick" that spat out fire and sudden death.

"We must go to Bill!" whispered Cliff. "We can't get out through the square! If we can get through the passages we may be able to hide." The others agreed. With the Inca, Huamachaco and Pizzara in hot pursuit, but unarmed, they almost leaped down the curving steps.

Bill stood at their foot, his back to them, his weapon leveled. Before him half a dozen soldiers hesitated.

"We're here!" cried Cliff. Then he saw Tom, just around the edge of the wall, tense and alert, his own light, and in this emergency almost useless weapon held ready.

If only they had known Tom was there, two minutes sooner!

Before they could make any concerted plan Pizzara, with his quick cunning serving him, caught old, weakened Mr. Gray by an arm: he saw that Bill could possibly daunt the soldiers; with merciless cruelty he dragged the old scholar past Bill before the others quite knew what he meant to do. Immediately he swung Mr. Gray, who was not strong enough to resist the surprise attack: Pizzara swung him so that his own body was shielded.

Bill saw, too late, the ruse. His weapon was useless: in that narrow place he could not fire without endangering the old student of ancient civilizations.

"Down, Father!" Cliff cried. "Drop down!"

The old man had recovered his balance. With all his small strength he tried to fling off Pizzara's grip, to lower his body. At the same instant the high priest and the Inca caught hold of Mr. Whitley and Bill. Cliff and Nicky in turn grasped them. Tom broke past Bill and caught a tackle around Pizzara's legs. His balance thus disturbed the Spaniard lost his grip on Mr. Gray.

Cliff tripped his adversary and with Mr. Whitley fighting with all his skill and science, soon was free to go to Tom's side.

Bill was there already, and a short-arm blow dazed the Spaniard. Down he went. But in that brief scuffle the soldiers had leaped forward.

Outnumbered, there was little that the desperate party could do. Pizzara shielded himself; a soldier wrestled with Bill for possession of the magic stick. It exploded once, but its muzzle was pointed toward the roof and no one suffered. During a lull in the scrimmage, for Cliff thought, in a passing flash, how like a football game was this scrimmage, the youth thought he saw Caya's brother holding a torch. But he was not sure.

Panting, perspiring, choked by the resinous smoke of the torches, the three men and their three youthful companions were soon overpowered. Bill's, and Tom's weapons, as well as those of Mr. Whitley—their only three pistols— had been flung to the floor.

Cliff made one valiant effort, rolling about with a soldier on his back, to grasp a revolver. But Pizzara kicked it aside.

"Into the dungeons!" cried the Inca.

Held by a soldier at either side, the six captives had no chance to try to make a break for liberty, even if such a try could have succeeded: with soldiers everywhere there was no chance for success.

Sombre and dejected, they were led to a place where guards moved aside great stones.

Into blackness, all together, they were flung!

CHAPTER XXVII
BEASTS OF BURDEN

Their dungeon was dark and it had the smell of an underground place, musty, damp, stuffy. When it seemed to Cliff that hours must have passed since they had all been flung into the single unlighted cubicle he looked at the radiumited face of the watch on his wrist: hardly half an hour had elapsed.

"This is truly a terrible situation," said Mr. Gray. "I feel very badly when I think that in coming here to help me you have all fallen into a worse situation."

"Please don't feel that way, Father," Cliff begged, touching the hand that trembled a little on his knee. "You always taught me that no good intention and no act done with a good motive could ever bring anything but good."

"It does not seem to work, this time," said his father.

"But it will!" Tom said. "Didn't you notice the soldier who walked with me? No, you didn't: I remember, we were behind you. Well, it was Caya's brother and he whispered to me to give him the quipu supposed to be the Inca's token."

"I didn't know that," Mr. Whitley spoke through the darkness. "He may try to help us."

"Mr. Whitley," said Nicky, "why can't we all push on that big stone across the door? It is on some sort of a pivot: we could all push together and move it."

"Yes, two of us could move it—the soldiers did," Bill took a part in the talk. "But the guards are outside. By the time we could get the stone moved they could use their swords."

"I guess we are helpless," Mr. Whitley said remorsefully. "And it is all my fault for letting you lads come here: you should have camped on the ledge: Bill and I should have taken the risks of danger."

"I still have faith that an Almighty Power watches over us," Cliff declared. "We have gone through a great deal of danger and not one of us has been hurt."

"I am proud of you, my son," said Mr. Gray. "And it is a rebuke to us who are older. I know, deep down in my heart, that you are right. After years among these people, unharmed, made nearly well when I thought my feebleness would destroy me, I should be thankful to that Great Power—and I am!"

"Let's all think 'we are going to get out all right,'" Nicky suggested. "Think as hard as we can."

No one replied. Perhaps, with all other help apparently denied them, they all had a mind to do as Nicky urged: at any rate the black room, with its air rapidly growing more stale and heavy, was so silent that they heard, through the place where the upper end of the barrier failed to touch the door frame, the muttering of several guards in the tunnel.

Ages passed, or so it seemed. In fact, hours did go slowly into the past, and nothing happened.

"Listen!" whispered Tom, finally, when the air had become so oppressive that they all began to feel heavy and dull. "Did I hear somebody walking?"

"Yes," answered Bill. "They are changing the guard, I guess."

"Poor Caya," said Cliff. "I feel sorry for her. She is all alone, in some hole as dark as this: and all on account of us."

"Yes," said Tom. "But she is alive—and so is her sister—because of us."

"I wonder where her brother is," Nicky mused.

"Sh-h-h!" warned Bill. "Be quiet and if the stone moves, let's all make a rush. I hear somebody fumbling at the stone."

He had moved close to the barricaded doorway in the dark. But as the stone began to move and they all gathered their muscles for a dash, they were chained with surprise.

"I am Pizzara," came the unmistakable voice of the Spaniard. "I come to help. Push there, you!"

The stone moved more and even the faint light from a torch jammed into a place made for it nearby in the tunnel wall was brilliant to their widened pupils. They blinked as they saw two figures, in the garb of the Inca's soldiers.

"It is Caya's brother and the stranger who spoke," said one of the figures, in quichua dialect. "Come forth quickly!"

They filed out; Nicky and Bill and Cliff helped support Mr. Gray who was stiff and tottering from his long inactivity. They saw Caya's brother tapping at several other door stones; finally he called to Tom and Cliff and the three managed to move a great barricade slowly a little way aside. Had it not been swung on a rude pivot this would have been impossible. As it was they got it far enough opened to allow Caya, shaking with excitement and eagerness, to come from her black prison.

"I meet this soldier," explained Pizzara. "I have watch him and I think he is friend. I ask him and it is yes. Now we go quick'."

"I certainly do beg your pardon," said Mr. Whitley. "I thought you were an enemy and you have liberated us."

The Spaniard showed his teeth in a curious grin.

"It is all a part of my plan," he said mysteriously as they went hastily along the passage, the young Peruvian carrying the single torch in the rear with his sister. "When you are sleeping in the lake bottom I steal away with my men. I think then we get here before you. But the Indians fling stones upon us in the white pass and my natives know it is danger'."

They kept careful watch but it seemed that no one was in the tunnels: the guards whom the Spaniard and the Indian had replaced had gone home or to their barracks and no one else was on guard, it seemed.

"All but one," the Spaniard went on. "My men are escape. I have gun and I make them go forward, but we go in old water way." The same one, Cliff mused, that they had used to get around the ambush; then he listened as Pizzara continued, "We find the ledge as it is on the map and there is your camp where you have leave some thing and the cord to haul the rope. It is very clever, *si*."

"You left your natives there," Bill said. "That's my guess. Then you came down into this valley. But how did you expect to get any gold—or much!—all alone?"

"Ah!" grinned Pizzara, "this one is clever, as you. I plan all this and as I plan so it is come out—just exactly."

"Plan?——" Cliff was puzzled. "How could you expect we would get into a dungeon and that you would save us—and what has that to do with your plan to get gold?"

"It is all simple," Pizzara grinned. "I come and see that you are here: then I find ways to make Inca suspect you, and high priest to make you prisoner. You help that by what you do. So then I have you where I wish to have you! It is good fortune of my patron Saint that this soldier and his sister are mix up with you. It make two more to carry for me."

"To carry?" demanded Mr. Whitley. "What do you mean?"

They had come to the place where the tunnel branched away in the direction of the break where the aqueduct used to flood the tunnels was situated: by common impulse they all swung after Tom who had memorized that way.

"Halt!" snapped Pizzara. They all stopped and looked at him. In the torchlight his face was a leering, triumphant mask of lustful delight. In his hand was the very "magic stick"—the small revolver—which he had caused the high priest to take from Bill when they were captured: Bill had not been able to use it, even in self rescue, for fear of shooting his friends; he had surrendered it with a scowl for his rifle, as he now knew, was in the hands of Pizzara's natives, waiting, at the camp on the ledge.

"We can't stop," Mr. Whitley said. "Some one may discover us."

You stop when I say!" Pizzara gloated, lifting the shining muzzle. "If I shoot you will be capture. I will escape and come another time to take the gold. If you do what I say you get way and I may give you one little bit of gold as a— a souvenir."

"You expect us to carry gold!—when we are trying to escape with Mr. Gray who is feeble?" Bill snapped at Pizzara.

"Yes!" replied Pizzara. "I have select gold that is carve very pretty: it is not too heavy with so many. It will sell very high for the art and not for the gold, as your scholar will say when he see what I have choose."

He lifted the revolver as Bill's fists doubled.

"You are a beast!" said Mr. Whitley. "A beast who——"

"Who drive beast of burden! Come and I load your backs!"

CHAPTER XXVIII
"CAN WE GET THERE IN TIME?"

Pizzara had been clever, indeed! He had so maneuvered the procession as they left the cells that Mr. Gray, the most feeble one, was in the lead and the Indian and his sister at the rear.

Therefore they could not make a dash for escape; and when they saw Pizzara's menacing look as he showed them that he also had his own revolver, a heavy, serviceable automatic, Mr. Whitley and Bill signaled submission. After all, it was their only chance for liberty.

"Look here," Bill turned on Pizzara. "You had better let the soldier and his sister escape—you can't ask them to rob their own treasure house. They think the Sun's gold is sacred!"

"I need them," said Pizzara. "The soldier have his father with rope to wait to help us at the cistern. If we have not these two how shall the others let us take the gold?"

"You are vile!" cried Mr. Gray. "To use them as hostages!"

"Cease grumbling, my little llamas," Pizzara said sarcastically. "Come and let the loads be put on your little backs—or!——" he crooked his trigger finger significantly.

The situation was too desperate for argument: when they sullenly filed into the room beneath the sun temple, Caya and her brother showed signs of mutiny but Bill whispered to them that if they raised an alarm there it would result in death for them all: he hinted that some way would be found to save the treasure—and they could take only a few choice carved and moulded pieces. Pizzara could not always be on guard.

Strangely enough the whites were all in sympathy with the Indians: they were not mercenary or lustful. The safety of Cliff's father, their own escape and a clear conscience were of more worth to them than the risk of a few thousand dollars and the feeling that they were thieves.

They were in such a situation that they had to help a thief but they felt sure that at some time when his vigilance was relaxed they could leave him to dispose of his gains, secured by coercion, as best he might.

He had chosen his loot wisely; they saw that as he indicated the lighter statues, beautifully worked, the animals, flowers and a few urns. He made them tear apart woolen weaves that were as fine and as soft as silk to make bundles and thongs with which to carry more than they could handle loose.

Cowed but sullen Caya and her brother did what they could to delay, but finally Pizzara had as much as he thought they could care for, and off they started, down the long tunnel, laden heavily. Even Mr. Gray, feeble as he was, had to carry the statue of Chasca, which weighed only about five pounds but which was a marvelously well wrought bit of purest gold: small though it was, for gold is heavy, every feature, every line, was perfect.

Herding them before him like the llamas he called them, Pizzara drove his bearers along, prodding the morose Indians with his two ready weapons.

They reached the outlet into the dry aqueduct: it was still a tunnel for the distance it ran under the temple gardens, but its stones were carefully fitted and joined with some hard, glasslike cement to help retain the water if the emergency ever arose in which it would inundate the underground ways: and, thought most of them, here was the emergency—if the truth were discovered by the Incas!

The first beginnings of dawn were in the Eastern sky when the party, their torch flung aside, came to the point where the water way was no longer under the gardens but ran, as an open, deep cut, to the mighty cistern which distributed the water from the mountain reservoirs.

"How are we going to get out of this?" Cliff asked as they saw the open sky through the slit of open stone above them.

"Caya's family waits with ropes near the cistern," Bill informed them all: he had learned of this from Pizzara who had allowed the young soldier to make his plans before he knew that the gold would be stolen; had Pizzara dropped a hint of his true purpose it is probable that the Indian would have tried to rescue his sister and then informed the Inca's troop of the Spaniard's plan; but Pizzara was cunning.

"But suppose they discover the escape?" broke in Nicky. "When do they change guards again, Bill—ask Caya!"

"It has been done already," Bill said. "I have asked her. That is why Pizzara is hurrying us. They must know that we are free and maybe they know that the gold is gone!"

"How far must we go?" Cliff asked.

"At least a mile."

"But won't they see us in this open aqueduct?"

"They probably won't waste time searching," Bill answered. "I expect that a chasqui-runner—has already been sent to the guards who handle the sluice gates."

Pizzara, himself, seemed anxious. He urged them to hasten.

"Look!" whispered Caya, clutching Cliff's arm. She pointed behind them. Against the growing illumination of the sky they saw a figure, slim, tall, standing out black against the sky, peering down at them. Suddenly he stood straight. Faintly they heard a hail and then the figure disappeared.

"That was a watcher," Bill said. "It's an even chance whether there are soldiers close enough to shower us with arrows, or whether they get those gates open before we reach the place where the rope will help us climb out."

They needed no prodding from Pizzara.

They ran over the loose pebbles and bits of loosened stone, stumbling, gasping, their lives in their hands; and yet, with all the danger, when Caya dropped her bundle Pizzara compelled her to stop and secure it.

"How can we get away, even if we do get out?"

Nicky panted as he asked the question. His bundle was getting heavier as the moments passed, and his excitement, even though it lent him strength, seemed to make the needless extra burden seem silly; he wanted to drop it, to run faster; but they could go no faster than they did because of Mr. Gray's feeble condition.

"If we can get to the place my father will help us with the rope," Caya said. "There is a great hole in the cistern, part way down. If we can get in there before the soldiers see us we can hide and they will not think of looking for us there."

"But won't the water drown us?" asked Cliff.

"I think it may not rise that high," she said. "But hurry—there we shall be safe!"

"Yes," Cliff panted. "If we can get there in time!"

CHAPTER XXIX
AT THE CISTERN

Although dawn was streaking the heavens with its colors, it was still dusk in the valley and pitch dark in their open cut.

"We are nearly there!" said Caya, coming forward in the dim line to help Cliff with his father: she took his statue in spite of her own burden and they hurried all they could.

From somewhere in the distance ahead they heard shouts.

"Can we make it?" panted Mr. Whitley.

"It's a question of minutes," gasped Bill. "Seconds, maybe! Hear that!"

As they neared the place where the great sluice gate of that particular distributing aqueduct was located they heard the shouting of men and the rumble of something—was it a huge stone being lifted by their rude and uncouth mechanical methods? Was that the gurgle of water they heard between the rumblings?

"Oh!" whispered Caya—"Here hangs the rope." She, in the lead, feeling the walls, had located something hanging down.

Her brother gave a sharp jerk, repeated it, was answered.

"Caya first," said Mr. Whitley.

"No," said Mr. Gray. "William—Bill first!"

"He can help pull up the rest," Cliff urged. "My father can't climb, he will have to be drawn up."

"Hurry, then, Bill," said Mr. Whitley. In the darkness they began to feel the rope twitch and jerk, and heard the scrape of boots feeling for a foothold on the fairly rough side of the aqueduct. Then, far up the side they saw, in the light from the reddening sky, Bill, monkeylike, climbing like a sailor.

Soon the rope came down again. There was a loop at its end. "Sit in the loop and hang on," Cliff and Mr. Whitley both urged.

"No," said Mr. Gray. "I am not going until the girl is safe." Caya was lifted for there was no time for argument. Bill and the eager father of the girl swung her in quick jerks upward.

Then the rope came down. "Wait!" said Pizzara. "Why not send the gold up now? I have tied the bundles together——"

A sharp push flung him aside. Mr. Whitley was at the end of his patience, seeing this man willing to risk their lives in preference to risking his gold. "You can send it up before you come," he said.

There was a more ominous rumbling close at hand and they began to swarm up the rope as soon as the old man was safe. But Pizzara hung back. The rest were climbing like sailors, for there came the sound of water beginning to seep around an obstruction and there was a tiny wet pool running along under foot. While they climbed Pizzara took his final chance with his Fate or luck or patron Saint's protection for he waited until he had made all the woolen thongs into a big knot and had swung that to the end of the rope: then he saw that he had no time to waste, for there was the beginning of a swirling torrent at his feet that swung him up and off his balance as he gripped the rope and began to surge upward. When his face topped the edge of a narrow step on which the others waited, he wore a sardonic grin which the growing light showed.

"I save the gold," he said. "Haul him up."

Cliff thought that Mr. Whitley was going to prevent that but Bill touched his arm: whispered, "Not yet—we will need the rope!"

They hauled up the gold, then, and were told to inch their way along the narrow ledge for a few feet to where, in the side wall, through long disuse, a great part had crumbled out, leaving a sort of rude cave, uneven of floor and jagged on its sides, but deep enough to enable them all to retire into the darkness at the back and be reasonably sure of not being seen. The rope was also out of sight and as they heard the roar of the waters rushing into the aqueduct, Cliff sighed.

"All that lovely woven stuff will be ruined," he said. "I feel ashamed of myself in a way for being partly the cause of so much destruction."

"It is Pizzara's fault, not yours," Nicky said. "If he hadn't touched the gold they might not have flooded the tunnel to stop us. If we had traveled light we could have been here sooner and we might have overpowered the gateman and prevented the opening of the gate."

"That is how to thank me when I save your life!" growled Pizzara.

"Little you cared for us," flared Nicky. "Only for the gold we could carry. You'll get paid back for that, some way."

Mr. Whitley's hand warned him to be silent. This was no time nor was it the place for quarreling or anger.

"Judge not——" he warned. "There is a Higher Power to attend to that, Nicky."

"Yes, you are right," Nicky admitted. "I'm sorry I spoke."

Caya's father had brought a little food, having had time to do no more when his son had raced home to plan with him for their rescue.

They ate and felt better.

"How do we get out of here?" Bill asked Caya's brother.

They must wait until night, he said, and then they could creep around the ledge to a place where there were steps, and if they could elude the guard there they could get to the level ground and make for the hills.

"But there is no way out of the valley when we get to them," objected Bill. "We don't know about the secret pass."

"Ah!" said Pizzara. "There, again, I am noble to save. I take you. When the high priest tell nobles to guard one place more than all other I follow. I shall save you even when you call me bad name."

Which only proved it true that one can never hate any man because it is never possible to tell when a seeming enemy may prove one's best friend. No matter how base Pizzara's motive might be, he was made an instrument in the hands of a higher power than hate, and he was to prove also that there is a law of exact justice, that what one gives, in his thoughts, whether love, hate, lust, envy, greed or generosity, it returns to him in some way and at some time.

The day was irksome, even with the thrills of seeing soldiers scouting around the reservoir: one even started to walk a little way along the ledge from the stairs of rough stone at the gates, but as the Incas had turned more water into the cistern and it was slowly raising the level toward the ledge he did not go far.

The water itself became a menace before night, for it was almost level with their small, deep cavern; but its rise was slow and would be unless some one cut off the flow into the tunnels, which must happen soon.

It would be a question for them of whether dark came before the water level flooded the break in the stone and swept them out into the cavernous cistern.

The water came almost to the edge and then receded as the gate to the reserve supply in the mountains was closed.

Then darkness came, and they started on the most perilous part of their journey, edging around the ledge. Fortunately for them it was dry and not slippery.

Again Pizzara showed that lust was stronger than caution for he elected to remain in the cavern until they got out; they were then to proceed to a point above the cavern, lower the rope and pull his gold and himself up that way.

They could not refuse for he knew the secret passes.

Finally they were all safe and again they resumed their golden burdens. Caya, who could not stay in the valley without danger of death when she was discovered, had decided to go with her brother, who was also endangered. Their plan was to seek her shepherd and his mother in the hills and to stay there for a while. Perhaps Caya might stay and make a home for him, who could say? She was shy as she said it. Bill told the others of the plans the Indians made, and they all turned away in sympathetic silence as Caya and her brother bade farewell to the stern, proud old father and the clinging, sobbing mother who had braved every danger of discovery to steal close enough to know that all was well and to say goodbye.

But in due time, they were done and again the party walked along under the stars, on open ground and in constant danger of detection—but, happily—perhaps because the Incas supposed that the tunnel flood had served its purpose—they were not seen.

Again, near daybreak, they were in the mountains, and well hidden in a deep crevasse into which light never penetrated.

CHAPTER XXX
A FORTUNE BY MISFORTUNE

"Who do you suppose that is?" asked Nicky, calling Cliff's attention to a slim figure standing not far from the point where the crevasse they were in opened onto the secret passway.

"Do you think it is a spy?" Tom whispered. They were still in hiding. Pizzara and Mr. Whitley had gone away early in the morning to try to find a way to get to their old camp on the ledge. Bill would have been the natural one to do scouting but it had been decided that he ought to stay to help the boys in case of danger of discovery. Although the crevasse, even in the middle of the day, was hidden in gloom that no sun's ray ever penetrated, and discovery was unlikely, there was the possibility that some Incas might intrude and discover the camp. In such a case Bill was better able to find a hiding place or to help the younger brains to find a course of procedure. But as the figure appeared at the mouth of the crevasse, Bill was fast asleep, worn out after the long exertion.

"Shall we call Bill?" asked Nicky.

"Wait," suggested Tom. "Keep perfectly still and see what he does."

But they had forgotten Caya. Rolled in her robe she had been asleep; suddenly, sitting up and staring, she leaped to her feet, cried out a name sharply and ran forward.

It was her shepherd of the hills. She quickly explained what so surprised him, her presence in the hills. Then she brought him to meet the younger members of the party. They liked him at once. He was a handsome, wind-browned, tanned Indian with clear, honest eyes and a likeable manner, though saying little.

He had been on his way the night before to meet Caya when he had found some of the soldiers at the secret pass; they knew him but told him to go and watch for the strangers if they had escaped to the hills; he had waited nearby and was wondering what to do and how to see Caya when she had seen him.

Mr. Gray and Bill were able to understand his hill dialect quite well and he took quite a liking to the kindly old scholar. But most of his time he spent with Caya, for he joined the camp as soon as he had gone away long enough to bring some food.

Late that night Mr. Whitley and Pizzara returned, leading the latter's Indians. They had found the camp on the ledge without much difficulty, there being an aqueduct that they could follow around the valley. They had all the food from both slender stores and all other equipment: the young men were very glad to get their American clothes again, and with a spare pair of corduroy trousers, an extra woolen shirt and Mr. Whitley's heavy coat they managed to outfit Mr. Gray in the first "civilized" garb he had worn for several years.

They planned to sleep in the crevasse: the next day the shepherd agreed to come again and bring more dried meat and corn for their journey and to show them the way to regain the regularly traveled mountain passes.

But when they awoke the next morning Cliff, Tom and Nicky observed the camp in dismay.

Pizzara had cheated them again. Once his natives were with him, rough half-breeds, more lustful for money than caring about honesty, he and they had "cleared out" during the night, taking everything belonging to both parties!

For once, however, his cupidity had led him astray.

When the young shepherd came to the camp the next day, soon after sunup, he told them that he had seen a strange thing: nearly a dozen men went silently along the secret way with packs. He rose and followed, thinking that his friends of the day before were leaving with Caya. Not knowing them he naturally did not trust them.

However, soon there came a shouting, the falling of rocks, the cries of injured men, the sharp flash of lightning from a long stick which one of the men held.

Thus the Indian described Bill's rifle which the Spaniard had stolen.

There was a loud noise after the flash, he said, and this happened several times: then the man fell down and there was much shouting and the tramp of feet marching along one of the higher ledges, with a chant of "Hailli—hailli!"

Bill and Mr. Whitley went to look at the place which the shepherd showed them. When they came back they were very sober and serious.

"Pizzara has stolen his last piece of gold," Bill told the eager chums. "It looks as though the Incas ambushed his party again—only this time the ambush was a complete success."

"Wiped out!" Mr. Whitley whispered to Mr. Gray.

"And how about the supplies?" Cliff asked.

"The Incas seemed to want to destroy the party: probably they think that the ones they attacked were our party. At any rate they used arrows, rocks and made a complete job of it. But they left the packs intact. It seems that they ambushed from above and did not even climb down to see anything."

"Then the gold is there too," Tom said.

"Yes," said Mr. Whitley.

Little more was said. They became thoughtful and silent.

"Caya and her brother are going with the shepherd," Bill said at length. "He will take them to his mother's little hut."

"I suppose Caya will marry him when she gets old enough," Tom said. "But what will her brother do?"

"He has listened to our talk about the wonders of our country," Mr. Gray said, "and he wants to stay with his sister until he knows she will be all right, and that, I suppose, means 'until she marries the shepherd,' then he will make his way to Cuzco. I have promised to send him some money, there, later on, and when he learns English and gets accustomed to the strange things that he will see everywhere outside his little hidden valley—who knows? He may come to visit us, some day!"

It was with considerable regret that the three chums said goodbye to Caya. She had been very faithful as a serving maid in the earlier days in the temple. Then she had endeared herself to their growing sense of chivalry by her sacrifice of freedom for their own sakes. They held her hand a little longer than was their habit with modern girls, and with no sense of sheepishness either!

Her brother they frankly made a comrade and if he did not understand their voluble promises of entertainment when he might come to see them at Amadale, they certainly conveyed a full sense of their comradeship to the straight young soldier.

Waving their hands, they watched Caya, her brother and the shepherd go out of sight down the crevasse and secret passway. Bill had a perfect route for their return tucked away in his pocket for he had drawn a rude map from the shepherd's directions.

When the three whose lives had so closely twined in with their own were out of sight Bill turned to Mr. Whitley.

"I don't know your mind and you don't know mine," he said—and the boys were tickled to hear the old expression he had used so often in the earlier days of their association—it seemed to bring them back to real, everyday things. "But to me it is a sin to leave that gold and those supplies to be ruined in the first storm in the mountains or to be buried in snow and ice this winter."

"We aren't stealing it," Nicky suggested. "It can't be returned to the Incas and the Spaniard—won't need it——"

Mr. Gray was so eager to take the highly valuable specimens of the ancient handicraft to civilization that he urged them also. Mr. Whitley did not so much object to taking the gold; he did not wish the young fellows to be exposed to the sight of the ambush: but Bill settled that by going with him to bring back the gold and such supplies as they could use.

And so, because of greed, Pizzara had acted as an instrument to save their lives and then had actually sacrificed his own and those of his natives; and those who had been, under his revolver, actually beasts of burden, became carriers of their own treasure.

And carry it they did, with no complaint, for the secret way which they traversed was by no means as terrible as that by which they had come. The Inca's way was cleverly chosen, cleverly hidden. But it was a very usable and easy way compared to the usual mountain passes.

One afternoon, as the sun was beginning to touch the tops of the Westward hills toward which the party now faced, they came to a narrow valley across which, far above, a swinging, osier-supported bridge was hung. But they did not cross the bridge; they went across the bottom of the valley and into a fissure in the rock that anyone would consider just one more cave, broken in there by Nature.

Nevertheless, it was not a cave but the opening into a great cleft in the virgin rock. Above them on both sides towered vast, steep granite slabs: their way lay between them.

Presently they came to steps, steep as a ladder almost, but firmly cut and shaped slightly downward at the inward side so that the wear of use leveling off the outer edge would not for centuries make the steps dangerous.

Up these they toiled, clinging dizzily, roped together, but not in any real danger. Mr. Gray, even, in spite of the toilsome journey, was in high spirits and, with many a rest but with a dauntless heart, he finally reached the top step and sat with his companions for a rest.

Soon they were off again: this time for only a short distance through a cleft; and when they emerged Cliff and Nicky gave a regular Indian war-whoop!

"See where we are?" shouted Cliff. "Look—yonder is the hut where I caught Huayca! There is the ledge where he watched our camp. This is the place, Father, where we lost the map and all———"

Sure enough! The Inca secret way had brought them out at almost the end of their journey; a few days and they would be in Cuzco, their adventures over!

That would have been the case if Huayca had not gone for a walk in the secret pass the day after the attack on Pizzara.

CHAPTER XXXI
CLIFF BECOMES A PROPHET

"This is a splendid place to stop until we can bleach out the copper color from our skins," Mr. Whitley suggested. "We will have to camp somewhere while Bill goes to the nearest settlement and gets something to take out this coloring: we left Cuzco as white people; we do not want to return in red skins."

"That will enable me to study this old ruin—I think it was a fortress," Mr. Gray added. "And, besides, I will admit that our last climb tired me greatly."

"Why can't we go where we had our camp before—down below?" Nicky inquired.

"We can guard this place better," Tom told him. "One man can watch that cleft we came from and we can loosen the osier ladder and draw it up: then no one can surprise us."

"Do you think anybody would try?" Nicky asked.

Cliff spoke up: he had been quite silent and thoughtful for many minutes.

"I vote to go on," he said.

Even Mr. Whitley looked at him in surprise.

"Why?" he asked.

"I have been thinking about 'Whackey,'" Cliff replied. "Something has kept reminding me of him ever since we began to make camp here."

"That is natural," Mr. Whitley explained. "That is because you captured him, strung him up by the heels, up here."

"Yes," Cliff admitted: then he frowned. "But that wouldn't make me feel as though he might be close to us now, would it?"

"Do you feel that way?" asked Bill.

Cliff nodded. "I keep thinking what I would do if I were in Whackey's place," he said.

"And what do you think you'd do?" Nicky demanded.

"This," answered Cliff. "Suppose me to be Huayca. Well, I slipped away and tried an ambush in the white pass and then reported to my ruler, the Inca. Then, a little later, I found out that my ambush had not frightened the white invaders away. Do you see what I am trying to make plain?"

"Yes," Tom nodded. "When the white invaders escaped from the dungeons and you heard about it, you might go with a party—or even lead it, as Whackey, of course—to destroy them if they were in the secret pass."

"How would he know that they were not drowned in the tunnel?" Nicky objected. "How could he believe they were in the secret pass?"

"Easy!" Cliff said. "We—the white invaders were seen in the open part of the aqueduct by a chasqui—remember? Well, that proved they were not drowned in the flooded tunnels. But they were not found in the aqueduct, either, when daylight came."

"That's so," Nicky agreed. "Then what?"

"Then—still pretending I am Huayca!—I would think they might have climbed out or someone might have helped—the Spaniard, maybe. The high priest might tell me that Pizzara knew about the secret pass or had heard of it. So I would go there."

"Well," said Bill, "that all fits in. Pizzara was caught during the night——"

"There!" cried Cliff, eagerly. "That is the point. It was at night! His band was wiped out. Now—if I were Whackey, I think I would go back there in daylight! And——"

"I see!" Tom put in. "Even at night the party could see that stuff was strewn all around. And in daytime—it was gone!"

"That is just what I mean!" Cliff was eager.

"By gravy!" Bill broke in, "I didn't even think about that. Of course the average Peruvian is no detective and might not go as deep as that. But he would wonder what happened to all the stuff!"

"Huayca was a very intelligent fellow," Mr. Whitley admitted. "If he did as Cliff said——" He stopped, thinking deeply.

"Then he might gather a party and follow us!" Nicky exclaimed.

"Why haven't they overtaken us sooner, then?" Bill asked. "They can travel faster than we did."

"Well," said Cliff, "still being Whackey, I think I would follow all by myself."

"Why?" It was like a chorus of well trained voices—all asked the question at one time.

"Less chance of being noticed for one thing. For another—and from what I saw of them I think this is how an Inca noble would think—I could let the party get to this ledge and make camp. Then I could wait until dark, slip over and cut away the ladder, wait until the camp was quiet to do it. Then I could pick them off, one by one, with a sling or bow and arrows, in the dawn. If any of the party hid in the ruins I could starve them out."

"And that is exactly the way an Indian's mind—an Inca, not an American Indian—would work," Mr. Gray nodded at Cliff.

"I prophesy that will happen if we stay here," Cliff said boldly.

And in all but one particular he was exactly right!

CHAPTER XXXII
THE ANDES CLOSE THEIR JAWS

The one thing in which Cliff did not outguess Huayca was in the manner of his planning for the white party's annihilation.

Huayca was not of the hidden Inca tribe. He was a man of Cuzco, but of the higher grade of intelligence. To him had come the Inca noble who had gone with Pizzara to America: that noble had chosen Huayca to serve him and had promised a great reward. By the failure of his ambush he had let the white party get through to Quichaka. And, worse, they had escaped again, as he discovered when he visited the scene of the night raid in the secret pass.

Huayca, being a native of Cuzco, knew that the Spanish justice was as swift as that of the Incas. Since he must live in Cuzco, far from Inca protection, he must not invoke the penalties which the Spanish law would demand if he destroyed the white party. Even in such a place as the Andes passes the law of the Americans would compel the law of the Spaniards to quest and to find him out, if he turned his hand against white men of that America.

He had a better plan and one so thoroughly diabolic that it seemed as though the Cupay, or evil spirit, of the Incas must have whispered it into his ear.

An infuriated mob, turning against white men who sought to rob the buried Incas, hidden among the hills, of their treasure—that was the instrument that would strike swiftly and who could seek, find or punish its scattered arms afterward? No one! Having followed the party to the stairway, keeping well hidden, he let them climb. He went to another spot in the secret pass and there, with catlike agility, soared up the side of a steep crag, hanging sometimes almost by a thread of sheer willpower, clinging with nails and bare feet; but he reached the top, slipped along it to another point, there descended to the main, open-traveled pass and so across the osier bridge. While Cliff was discussing his prophetic idea Huayca ran fleetly along the main pass, under the lip of that very ledge, bound for the nearest settlement.

Bill, when Cliff made his prophecy, looked very sober.

"You may be right," he told Cliff, "but here's our situation: We can't go back to Cuzco as Indians. If we leave this ledge we lose a good position, in the matter of strategic location; no one can attack us from below if we cut loose the ladder and we can guard the cleft much easier than we could watch an open place on the pass. I vote for staying here, at least until I can get some stuff to replace the bleacher we lost when Pizzara took our packs away."

They talked it over from every angle and finally, although Cliff felt that he was right, they found no other plan as good as Bill's. Having their strong, light rope, plenty long enough to reach the ground, they promptly cut loose the upper fastenings of the Incas's osier ladder and put a guard, in two-hour shifts, just within the cleft, with Bill's small revolver, recovered from Pizzara by Bill after the visit to the scene of the Spaniard's destruction: a shot would warn the whole camp, day or night.

They ate a frugal supper for the supplies were running very low and must be made to last at least a day more, until Bill could visit the settlement and come back with more. Then, because it was cold and they did not wish to build a fire to attract attention, they made rude blanket beds within the small stone hut, and, secure in the knowledge that Nicky was wide awake, watchful, in the cleft, they slept with the healthy weariness of their long climb that afternoon.

And beyond their camp the mighty Incas were getting ready to snap their jaws and leave the white party, apparently, no way of escape!

At ten o'clock Nicky left his post long enough to shake Bill awake: it was Bill's next watch. The mountain prospector woke easily, got up, already alert and rested, and took up his post.

And the mountains seemed to sleep.

Mr. Whitley's watch, from midnight till two, was equally uneventful. Mr. Gray was spared a watch the first night and so it was Cliff who was called to follow Mr. Whitley.

Huayca, having gone to a small settlement, called the men in council, told them that the white men who had previously gone that way were coming back, disguised as Indians, and thus fired his fuse to ignite Peruvian hatred. He told them that the men had discovered an old burial mound, far in the hills, and had ravaged it, in spite of his protest.

Then, giving them some hints, he slipped away, leaving a fuse of anger steadily hissing toward a powder-keg of rage and racial hatred.

Huayca, feeling quite happy, returned along the pass, over the bridge, up the cliff, along its top, down into the valley spanned by the bridge, and thus again up the stone stairway that Cliff's party had used the afternoon before: he was back in the narrow outlet by the time that Cliff, consulting his radiumite watch face, decided to call Tom for his shift just after Cliff's own ended.

It was so still, Cliff thought, that you could almost hear the stars singing as they twinkled with strange brightness in the clear air.

Not a sound reached Cliff's ears, though. The stars did not sing, nor did anything else make any noise. Nature seemed to be resting in the wee hours before dawn, gathering her strength for a new day.

So Cliff crept as quietly as he could to the hut and shook Tom.

When his chum was thoroughly awake and stood outside the doorway with him, Cliff spoke.

"Don't shoot if you see a shadow on the ledge," he said in a whisper. "I am going over to the edge and look around toward the lower pass for a minute before I roll into my blanket."

"All right," Tom agreed, and went one way while Cliff went the other.

Tom comfortably disposed just inside the open fissure, saw Cliff standing outlined against a star. The cleft was as still as a tomb. Tom gazed up at the stars, looked along the deep, velvety blackness of the fissure, turned to look again toward Cliff.

Something was happening!

Cliff seemed to be moving crazily—or was it Cliff and another.

Tom deserted his post and raced across the turf. Then he shouted, pointed his small revolver aloft, pressed the trigger.

Crash! And the camp started up. The jaws had shut and the Andes were ready to crunch their prey.

CHAPTER XXXIII
NO WAY OUT?

While Cliff went to call Tom, Huayca, not too far away up the cleft, slipped closer and when he saw Cliff disappear into the gloomy ruin he whipped across the grass and into hiding at the ruins themselves.

He was within the guarded zone, therefore, when Tom took up his vigil.

But Cliff's move to the ledge surprised Huayca. Also, it annoyed him: it might disrupt his plans. He counted on a surprise. He desired to remain silent until dawn, while men from the settlement crept up the pass. At dawn his plan was to shout and begin firing arrows into the camp. Then they would rush for the ladder and so plunge down into the arms of the men who would then be waiting in the pass.

But Cliff, as Huayca could tell when he crept close, flat on his stomach— Cliff was watching something. Perhaps one of the men had a light—down in the pass!

As Cliff turned, alarmed by whatever he saw, Huayca, a panther in quickness and a shadow in the gloom, leaped!

He got a hand over Cliff's mouth.

Then Tom came running, there was the shot. Huayca tried to fling Cliff away, to escape and hide; but Cliff, too, had determination. He clung to his assailant!

Then, at the shot, there rose from the pass the angry, ominous roar of many voices.

The Andes growled over their prey!

Everybody was awake on the higher level. They all came running, Tom first. He caught Huayca in a tackle that helped to upset both struggling adversaries; but, striking sideways, he sent them to the turf with Cliff uppermost. Nicky piled on, then, and there was no chance of Huayca rising right away, squirm though he might.

Bill, when he came pelting, wasted no time: he saw the gleam of bright steel, for Huayca's knife came from Spain. Bill saw that it was no time for niceness. He kicked Huayca's wrist and with his screech of a wounded leopard Huayca's wrist became limp; Bill snatched the weapon from the ground.

Mr. Whitley was there by that time. It took very little longer to trice up Huayca, a snarling, defeated Indian.

They peered over the ledge cautiously, but there was nothing to see: the pass was like a deep well, jet black, impenetrable. They dragged Huayca back to the hut, tried to force from him the secret of the pass, but he would not speak. Bill hinted at some methods a little more forceful but both Mr. Gray and Mr. Whitley demurred. Dawn would soon be upon them: they were all wide awake, and, dividing into two groups, one with Bill's rifle, the other with two revolvers, each led by the older men, they watched at the cleft and near the ledge.

Beneath them those on the ledge could hear mutterings and growls, as of angered animals.

"It sounds as though there were lions down there," said Nicky.

"What puzzles me about the affair, tonight, is: How could Huayca get past us and go down the pass?" Cliff said. "Or—if those people down there are from Quichaka—how they got past us."

It was dawn before they discovered the reality.

Then Bill, looking carefully over, to be greeted with a flung stone which, however, did not reach the ledge, made a statement.

"There are forty men down there," he said. "They are not from Quichaka. They are men of some settlement: I can tell by their clothes."

"Then Huayca must have passed us," Cliff declared. "But how?"

"There must be another way around this ledge," Mr. Whitley said.

"If we could find it——" Tom did not finish. It would give them a chance to escape, was the thought in his mind. But Bill shook his head.

"If they know it they are watching it," he assured his friends.

One of the men on the lower road shouted up at them.

"Oho!" Bill said, interpreting. "He says for us to give ourselves up. He calls us robbers. Huayca must have gotten past us and told about the gold."

"Then let's give them the gold and go," suggested Mr. Whitley.

"Giving them the gold won't help. They are furious. Whackey must have said we robbed some tomb. That's what I make out of that fellow's yelling."

"Then we are trapped," Mr. Gray said.

"Looks like it," Bill admitted. "But they can't get up from where they are any more than we can get down—all we have to do is double-guard the cleft."

"Until they starve us out," said Nicky ruefully.

It seemed as though that was the intention. If the men on the road could not reach them, hunger would.

"Is there no way out?" Mr. Whitley said, at noon. He felt the responsibility he had incurred for the safety of his young charges. But no one gave him any answer.

CHAPTER XXXIV
HUAYCA PLAYS DECOY

"This is how the situation shapes up," Bill said, finally. "We could wait until dark and then attract their attention to the place, around the pass bend, where the ladder was: get them all there, waiting for us to come down, while we sneak down the rope out of their sight on the far side and run for it.

"The objection," he went on, "is that when they discover that we are running down the pass they can run after us and most likely they can overtake us."

"What we want to do," Cliff said, "if we can, is to get them somewhere that we can cut them off."

"That's talking!" Bill agreed. "But where?"

"Well, if we could have them come up here while we went down," Nicky began. Then he shook his head for he saw that his idea was rather impossible.

"The way everything is laid out here," Cliff declared, "it keeps them from us but it keeps us from getting away. If we could just get them to cross that osier bridge over the gulf, we could cut the strands of the support and that would block them for good."

The bridge he referred to spanned the chasm from one side of it, where the pass they were above ended, to the other, where another path began.

That was the way they had gone toward Quichaka. Returning the secret way, they had gone through the bed of the chasm, with the bridge over their heads, to one side.

"If there was some way to get from the gulf up to the pass on the far side——" Tom said. "There must be. That would account for Whackey getting past us to see the men who are yelling at us right now."

Bill said that there must be such a way and he took his larger revolver and set out, up the cleft, toward the steep steps. If a man had gone from the chasm up to and across the bridge, he would see some signs and find a way, he declared.

The party passed the intervening time throwing stones to keep the lower enemies interested. Had they been able to surprise the antagonists it would have been easy to stone them away, as the Incas had no doubt done in the old days. But the men on the pass were on their guard and had taken refuge close under the lip of the ledge which overhung the pass a trifle. To fling stones accurately the chums would have had to look far over and invite arrows or possibly bullets if any of the men of the mountain settlements carried arms. The stones were flung simply to keep the others close under the ledge until Bill's reconnoitering trip was finished.

"Here he comes!" cried Nicky, just before the sun dropped behind the peaks and sent the lower levels into a deep gloom.

"And he has found it," cried Tom. "I can tell by his face."

Bill had, indeed, found the way taken by Huayca previously. He explained the method to them.

"But it doesn't help us any, as far as I can see," he said. "If we went that way we would still have those fellows between us and safety."

But Cliff took him aside and whispered: then they came back and the entire party discussed a plan Cliff had thought out.

Huayca sullenly refused to obey when Bill shortly ordered him to get moving. Bill, carrying out Cliff's idea, compelled Huayca, his own knife pricking the back of his neck, to go ahead of his tormenter, along the path through the cleft.

"Keep them interested," Bill urged. "Light dry brush and throw it down. Do anything you can think of to make them sure you are up here—for half an hour. Then—just keep still until I get back."

He drove the disgruntled and frightened Indian before him, down the steep steps. Bill had a flashlight and was able to prevent the bound arms from doing him any injury: in fact, Huayca had enough to do, keeping ahead of the pricking point of his knife, as he clung to the bracing osiers along the steps, with just enough loose rope between his wrists to enable him to help himself.

It would have been foolhardy to try to make Huayca climb the cliff on the far side of the chasm, as well as to get down the other cliff to the far end of the bridge.

Cliff's plan was otherwise arranged.

Once in the chasm, Bill forced Huayca ahead of him until they had crossed the deep gulf.

There, in the shelter of a clump of brush almost under the end of the osier bridge he compelled Huayca to sit down: Bill bound him securely in that position. Then he walked a few feet away and gathered some small twigs and a few larger sticks. With those he made ready a fire. Once it was ignited and began to blaze he fired his revolver twice.

That was the signal. Those on the ledge grew tense. Bill—good old Bill!—had done his part. He was racing back across the chasm toward the steps. In

an hour or a little more he would be in their midst. But—in the meanwhile!—
—

The men on the pass heard the shots. They began to look around. Where had they come from? They knew what firearms were. But the sound had not come from the ledge above them: indeed, the people on the ledge had been so quiet that it might be that they had gone—if there was any way for them to go. And there was: the mountaineers knew there was a cleft in the walls above that ledge.

One of them ran around the bend in the pass and shouted, pointing. They all rushed in his direction.

Far below, and in the extreme distance of the chasm's far side, they saw a tiny fire and what might be a man sitting near it.

The ones on the ledge, then, they argued hastily, had used the passage through the cleft and down the old Inca steps.

They must be over the chasm, camped there, thinking they were safe because there was no way to get at them. The men who hated them and sought their lives could not climb to the ledge and get to them through the cleft: but there was another way to reach them, camped there in the chasm.

Stones! Stones would reach that camp!

The men, shouting like wild things heated by the lust of the kill, snatched up hands full of large stones: several even lugged large boulders.

It was a bad time for Huayca—or it would have been only that Bill, more kindly than the Indian would have been, had adjusted the bonds so that strenuous effort would loosen them after a while.

Over the bridge of swaying planks raced the exultant mountaineers with their missiles; and Huayca, realizing at last what the queer situation meant to him, redoubled his efforts to loosen his hands so that he could free his bound feet.

Down the ladder, which they had saved and drawn up when it had been cut free, went Tom, Nicky, Mr. Whitley and Cliff.

Two of the enemy had not reached the bridge; they turned as they saw the youthful trio and man drop down the side of the ledge; but Cliff and Tom, first down, plunged at them so menacingly in the dark that they ran out a ways on the bridge.

Mr. Whitley carried an axe, and Tom and Cliff and Nicky all had strong claspknives.

While the men on the bridge wondered, hesitated, those far toward the other side were pelting the campfire in the chasm with their rocks, shouting and yelling so that they did not hear the warnings of their comrades whom Nicky held off with the rifle because Mr. Whitley was swinging the axe with steady, telling strokes.

Crunch! Smash! Crumble!

One strand of the two great cables supporting the bridge planks was cut.

Then the men saw what was happening and turned to rush back across the swaying, teetering, weakening structure.

But Tom and Cliff were hacking away the smaller twists of osier so that soon there was a space several feet wide where there was no support for the planks.

Crack! Crack! Crunch! Crash!

Mr. Whitley was cutting through the osier on the other half of the swinging bridge. The more deliberate Mr. Gray had by now come down the ladder and he held up a torch for them to see by.

The light served to show the men on the bridge how dangerous was their situation. Any minute the second strand might part and the end of the bridge would then go swinging down—down——

In terror, stumbling over one another, pushing, screaming, they made for the far side of the bridge, which was naturally the nearer to them, for safety.

Mr. Whitley withheld his axe until he was certain that there were no more men on the bridge.

Crash! Two or three more blows and the bridge, weakened and strained, parted and went crashing down.

Between them and their enemies yawned a bridgeless chasm. Long before the men could get up one cliff, over and down, across the valley where they found the terrified Huayca hiding, up the steep stone stairway and onto the ledge, Cliff, Nicky, Tom, Mr. Whitley, Mr. Gray, and Bill—who had come back safely, were on their way toward Cuzco.

And this time their adventures were truly over and they had plenty of time to disguise their golden burdens, to bleach off their dye where it would show, and to return to civilization, satisfied for the time being that the Mystery Boys had saved a white man from eternal captivity and, in the bargain, brought out a nice collection of golden treasure!

CHAPTER XXXV
FOLDED ARMS

"Amadale is going to be tamer for us, than a sick rabbit," volunteered Nicky. He and Tom and Cliff were once more in the couch swing on Aunt Lucy's porch.

But this time no mysterious Spaniard, no queer Indian faced them. Instead, a tall, lanky, lean-jawed man with a likeable grin squatted on the floor, idly whittling to a satiny finish a long piece of wood. Had the chums looked through the living room window they could have seen Mr. Gray, Cliff's father, entirely restored to health, showing his collection of Inca treasures to three scholars. Mr. Whitley, tilted back comfortably in a chair, its back against the porch rail, smiled at Nicky.

"First class in History—and ancient history at that!—begins tomorrow," he chuckled. "Thomas, please tell me what Inca is the most famous."

"Whackey!" grinned Tom. "He gave America back its citizens."

"And now, Nicholas, what was the empire of the Incas most famed for?"

"Adventure!" promptly replied Nicky.

"Cliff," continued the instructor, carrying on his joke, "You next. What fact will you remember most about the Incas?"

"My father's rescue," said Cliff seriously.

That rather ended the joke for they all became sober as they recalled how much danger they had faced to save him.

"I told you we'd come out all right if we all thought we could!" Nicky said.

"We came out better than all right!" declared Tom, fondling the bright tan colored and brand new bank pass book in which his share of the treasure showed as a sizeable deposit.

The treasure they had managed to get to Cuzco had been so cleverly packed in among their old dunnage that the sleepy officials who had no idea that these men had been among fabulous treasures did not even bother to examine their old packs, and so, although there would have been a large part of the beautifully wrought objects claimed by the Peruvian government, none was noted and they got it all through. In America, because of its value as art objects and because they did not intend to dispose of any of it for profit, there was no duty charged.

Their share of the revenue came from the purse of Cliff's father. While he did not buy the gold directly from them, to each he gave a substantial sum for deposit. Mr. Whitley had been reimbursed for his expenditures and had refused to take a cent more. Bill, though, had accepted a good amount with which to buy the ranch for which he yearned. For Mr. Gray, scholar and writer of many books, found on his return to America that his volumes already written had brought in a steady royalty and for a series of articles on the life and customs of the Incas he received a large cash payment.

They had agreed not to disclose to the world the actual adventures they had experienced: also, each was bound by the most solemn oath of the Mystery Boys not to divulge the fact that the Incas still lived in their valley.

To do so, Mr. Gray urged, would send a host of adventurers—or worse—to invade the hills and to rob and harm the Incas. Instead they let it be understood that the scholar had been on an expedition, had found some valuable old things in the hills and had secured them for the gift which he made of them to a National museum.

Bill was visiting the four comrades who, with Cliff's father, had endeared themselves to him. Soon he would go further West to pick out a good ranch location.

"I wonder if Bill will find it as much excitement chasing steers and branding them as he found it rescuing my father?" Cliff said.

"Nope!" answered Bill. "But don't forget—I'm one of the Mystery Boys still. One of these days I expect there will be a letter coming by airmail to my ranch—'Dear Bill, come a-riding! We're going to try to find Tom's sister and discover what that cipher is that Nicky's got.'"

"Why must we wait?" urged Nicky. "We're all here now!"

"There is school!" reminded Mr. Whitley.

"Yes," agreed Nicky. "But it will be tame after the Incas."

"But we can do one thing," Tom broke in. "We can decide how to go about finding out what's in Nicky's cipher, can't we?"

"I think it will be wiser to wait until our heads are free from lessons," smiled Mr. Whitley. "I, for one, cannot go on any further quest for treasure until I have fulfilled my contract with the Amadale Academy."

"Well," said Nicky, the irrepressible, glancing at his friends as, out of the corner of his eye he saw Aunt Lucy within the living room, approaching the window with a big plateful of cakes and a pitcher of lemonade. "Well, I know one thing we can decide on, right now."

"What?" they all asked him.

Nicky grinned. Gently he began stroking his left ear with the middle finger of that hand. It was the call for a council.

Promptly, and somewhat curiously, Tom, Cliff, Bill and Mr. Whitley sat with folded arms—the sign that they were in readiness.

The Mystery Boys were again in council.

"You'll promise on the oath, 'Seeing All, I see nothing: Knowing All, I know nothing: Telling All, I tell nothing'——?"

"Certainly we'll promise!" said Tom impatiently. "What is it, Nicky?"

"I know!" cried Cliff, as Aunt Lucy stood, smiling, at the window, "We've got to decide a great question!"

"What?" asked Bill.

Grinning from ear to ear Nicky pointed to his watch, then jammed a finger toward his open mouth—and grabbed a cookie!

"When do we eat?" he shouted.

They all laughed and each elevated his right hand to rub his stomach.

"Now!" they replied.

And the council of the Mystery Boys was dissolved!

THE END